ENOUGH OF SORROW

More by Lawrence Block

WRITING AS JILL EMERSON

SHADOWS • WARM AND WILLING • ENOUGH OF SORROW • THIRTY • THREESOME • A MADWOMAN'S DIARY • THE TROUBLE WITH EDEN • A WEEK AS ANDREA BENSTOCK • GETTING OFF

NOVELS

A DIET OF TREACLE • AFTER THE FIRST DEATH • ARIEL • BORDERLINE • BROADWAY CAN BE MURDER • CAMPUS TRAMP • CINDERELLA SIMS • COWARD'S KISS • DEAD GIRL BLUES • DEADLY HONEYMOON • FOUR LIVES AT THE CROSSROADS • GETTING OFF • THE GIRL WITH THE DEEP BLUE EYES • THE GIRL WITH THE LONG GREEN HEART • GRIFTER'S GAME • KILLING CASTRO • LUCKY AT CARDS • NOT COMIN' HOME TO YOU • RANDOM WALK • RONALD RABBIT IS A DIRTY OLD MAN • SINNER MAN • SMALL TOWN • THE SPECIALISTS • SUCH MEN ARE DANGEROUS • THE TRIUMPH OF EVIL • YOU COULD CALL IT MURDER

THE MATTHEW SCUDDER NOVELS

THE SINS OF THE FATHERS • TIME TO MURDER AND CREATE • IN THE MIDST OF DEATH • A STAB IN THE DARK • EIGHT MILLION WAYS TO DIE • WHEN THE SACRED GINMILL CLOSES • OUT ON THE CUTTING EDGE • A TICKET TO THE BONEYARD • A DANCE AT THE SLAUGHTERHOUSE • A WALK AMONG THE TOMBSTONES • THE DEVIL KNOWS YOU'RE DEAD • A LONG LINE OF DEAD MEN • EVEN THE WICKED • EVERYBODY DIES • HOPE TO DIE • ALL THE FLOWERS ARE DYING • A DROP OF THE HARD STUFF • THE NIGHT AND THE MUSIC • A TIME TO SCATTER STONES

THE BERNIE RHODENBARR MYSTERIES

BURGLARS CAN'T BE CHOOSERS • THE BURGLAR IN THE CLOSET • THE BURGLAR WHO LIKED TO QUOTE KIPLING • THE BURGLAR WHO STUDIED SPINOZA • THE BURGLAR WHO PAINTED LIKE MONDRIAN • THE BURGLAR WHO TRADED TED WILLIAMS • THE BURGLAR WHO THOUGHT HE WAS BOGART • THE BURGLAR IN THE LIBRARY • THE BURGLAR IN THE RYE • THE BURGLAR ON THE PROWL • THE BURGLAR WHO COUNTED THE SPOONS • THE BURGLAR IN SHORT ORDER

KELLER'S GREATEST HITS

HIT MAN • HIT LIST • HIT PARADE • HIT & RUN • HIT ME • KELLER'S FEDORA

WRITING AS JILL EMERSON

Shadows

Warm and Willing

Enough of Sorrow

Thirty

Threesome

A Madwoman's Diary

The Trouble With Eden

A Week as Andrea Benstock

Getting Off

ENOUGH OF SORROW
Copyright © 1965 by Lawrence Block
Original Publication, writing as Jill Emerson
ISBN - 978-1-954762-14-5

Cover & Interior by JW Manus

A LAWRENCE BLOCK PRODUCTION

JILL EMERSON #3

Enough of Sorrow

LAWRENCE BLOCK

Chapter 1

The girl's name was Karen Winslow. She was tall and slender, with dark brown hair and eyes just a shade lighter. She was not a beautiful girl. Her jawline was too hard, her nose a little too long. But she might have been pretty. Prettiness does not depend upon perfect features. If she had held herself properly, if her step were firm, if her eyes were bright and her lips curled in a smile, she would have been pretty. She had been pretty in the past, so gently pretty as to seem quite beautiful at first glance.

She was not pretty now. Her pale lips were a straight line and her eyes were dull, almost opaque. Her whole body sagged as she walked, as though she were literally dragging herself through the grayness of the afternoon. She neither looked nor felt pretty.

At the corner of Second Avenue and Fifth Street she stopped and leaned against the side of a weathered brick building. She couldn't seem to catch her breath. She breathed deeply, closed her eyes, exhaled, took another breath, let it out, opened her eyes again. She was dizzy and she thought she was going to fall down or be sick or both. She wanted a cigarette badly. She fumbled through her purse, found a pack of cigarettes. It was empty. She stood there, still leaning against the building, and she held the empty cigarette pack in her hand and stared at it for a full minute. A woman stopped pushing a shopping cart long enough to ask her if something was wrong.

"Wrong?" She wanted to laugh. "No," she said slowly. "Nothing's wrong, only my pack is empty, that's all."

The woman started to say something, then changed her mind. Karen crumpled the pack slowly and let it fall to the sidewalk. There was a drugstore on the other side of Second Avenue. At the tobacco counter she asked for a pack of Marlboros. The clerk gave her a pack and took half a dollar from her and gave her a dime.

She remained in front of the counter while she opened the pack. She removed four cigarettes, put one between her lips and dropped the other three into her purse.

"I won't need the rest of these," she said.

The clerk looked at her.

"I'll probably only smoke one or two," she said. "Four at the very most. So I won't need the others."

"We don't sell 'em one at a time, honey."

"Oh, I know," she said quickly. "I didn't want a refund or anything." She pushed the pack across the counter to him. "It's just that I won't need these," she said. "You keep them. Smoke them yourself if you want. Or give them to somebody."

She left him standing there with an uncertain look on his face. She walked out of the drugstore and headed downtown on Second Avenue, the cigarette still hanging unlit from her lips. Halfway down the block she remembered the cigarette and stopped in a doorway to light it. The third match worked, and she drew smoke into her lungs and felt dizzy and nauseous all over again. She swayed, then shook off the feeling and began walking once more.

At the corner of Stanton Street she stopped to toss the cigarette into the gutter. She looked across the broad avenue and scanned the block for the building where she had lived so long. But it was gone, it and the tenements on either side. Now there was a vast hole in the ground where the buildings had been, and soon, according to a large sign, there would be a housing project erected on the site.

She closed her eyes and remembered the building, remembered their apartment on the fifth floor. A drab, joyless building, a cold and sterile apartment of three small rooms and a kitchenette, cracked plaster, cooking smells in the rooms and stale beer smells in the stair-well. How long had she lived there?

When she was six they had moved there from another apart-ment she could not recall at all. And they had moved out five years ago, and she was twenty-two now. Eleven years in that apartment, and now it was gone, the whole building gone.

She lit another cigarette. There were two left in her purse now. She gazed again at the empty lot. Everything was gone now, she thought. Her father had died in that apartment, and she and Ted and her mother had moved out while his coughing still echoed against the walls. And then her mother died in their new apartment in Parkchester, and now Ted was somewhere in the South—Texas, Louisiana, Fort Something-Or-Other, drafted and packed and gone. Gone, gone, gone, everyone, everything. The family, the building, ev-erything gone, and she was alone and lost.

Now Ronnie was gone, too.

She closed her eyes and tried to bring his image into focus. But it was blurred, fuzzy around the edges, elusive as a childhood memory. Only the lips, curled in a smile that was not a smile at all.

"I think this is where I get off, Karen. But don't think it hasn't been fun . . ."

She had cried, and he had left, and then her tears stopped and since that time she had not cried at all.

She dropped the cigarette and crushed it underfoot She had only taken a few puffs on it and she decided that it did not matter—she had two left and two would be more than enough. She turned away from the empty lot where she had lived once, went another block down Second Avenue, turned again on Rivington Street.

The candy store was still here. She looked in through the fly-specked window for Mr. Reuben, but Mr. Reuben was gone and a Puerto Rican with a bushy black moustache stood behind the counter. All of the stools were empty. She opened the door and went inside and ordered a chocolate egg cream. That was what she had always ordered at Mr. Reuben's store. The man made her an egg cream and she looked at it for a moment, then tasted it. She tried to remember whether or not it tasted the same as egg creams had tasted before and it seemed very important to know whether it did or not. And then she decided that it wasn't important at all. She paid a dime for the egg cream and put it down unfinished.

"I don't need this," she said. "There's nothing wrong with it, you see, but I just don't want it, that's all."

The man did not understand. He said something in Spanish, and she looked at his dark eyes and bushy moustache and turned and fled.

Halfway down Rivington Street a sign said ROOMS 4 RENT. She went into a dark hallway and rang the bell marked SUPERINTENDENT. She waited, and after a few moments an old lady came down the hallway toward her, a fat-bottomed old lady who walked as though she had lead in her shoes.

Karen said, "I'd like a room, if you have one, please."

"One on the second floor. No cooking, and the bathroom's down the hall."

"That's fine."

"It's six dollars a week."

"I just wanted it for tonight."

"We rent by the week."

"Listen, I'll pay you six dollars, do you understand? But I just want the room for tonight."

The old woman's eyes narrowed. "Six dollars you could take yourself and go to a hotel."

"I just wanted—"

"This is something funny, you and the room?"

"No, I—"

"I can't charge you six dollars, not for a night. You got three dollars? Give me three dollars and you can have the room."

She found three dollar bills in her purse and gave them to the woman. There was also a five-dollar bill in the purse, lying loose in the bottom of the bag, and there was a ten-dollar bill rolled up tight and kept in an empty lipstick tube. With all that money, she realized, she could have gone to an expensive hotel. Some elaborately clean place, where they carried your bags for you and there was a phone in your room and air-conditioning.

"No baggage?"

"Pardon me? I wasn't—"

"I said you got no baggage?"

"Oh, no. No, I don't."

The woman shrugged and showed her to the room. It was on the second floor in the rear, a small room, a wall of beaverboard to show that the room had been created by dividing another larger room in half. The room was furnished with a narrow bed and a chest of drawers. Little else would have fit into it.

"Good enough for you?"

"Fine."

The woman cleared her throat and went away. Karen listened to her footsteps as she lumbered slowly downstairs. She sat on the edge of the narrow bed and smoked the third of her four cigarettes, and she looked out the little window at the rear wall of another tenement. There was a shade on her window, yellow, ripped here and there and curling at the edges. She drew the shade and went back to sit on the edge of her bed again.

She finished the cigarette and left the fourth one in her purse. Then she reached into the purse and took out a package of five safety razor blades. She tried to remember when she had bought them. Today was . . . what? Thursday or Friday, she wasn't sure which. And she had bought the blades the night she had seen the movie, and she couldn't remember the title, and she had seen the movie that weekend, probably on Sunday. Was that right?

It hardly mattered.

Ronnie had left on a Thursday. That had been either two or three weeks ago, and she could not possibly remember which. She remembered that it was a Thursday, though, because she remembered going to the doctor Tuesday to find out one way or the other, and being scared to tell him Tuesday night and all day Wednesday, and finally telling him Thursday after he had asked her what was the matter with her.

So she had told him either two or three weeks ago to the day. It seemed funny to know something like that to the day but not to the week, like knowing that the battle of Hastings was fought on October 14th, but not knowing the year.

She knew dates, like the battle of Hastings. October 14, 1066. And the battle of Malplaquet. September 11, 1709. And Nelson's victory at Trafalgar. October 21, 1805. Most people couldn't remember dates like those at all, and some could remember only the year, but hardly anyone could remember the whole date without having made a special effort to memorize it in the first place. She could, though. And even now she didn't forget that sort of thing. It stayed with her.

She could remember the month and day and year that Marlborough and Prince Eugene won at Malplaquet, but she couldn't say for sure whether today was a Thursday or a Friday.

She opened the pack of razor blades, took out one of the five, unwrapped it. She put the little scrap of paper in which the blade had been wrapped into her purse, along with the four remaining blades. Another loose end, she thought. Four leftover blades, like the one leftover cigarette and the fifteen leftover dollars. She wondered if perhaps she ought to make a will, a very legalistic document full of whereases and heretofores.

I, Karen Winslow, being of sound mind, do hereby bequeath fifteen dollars and four razor blades and a Marlboro cigarette to whoever wants it.

No, that wouldn't do. She wasn't of sound mind, and the courts would throw it out.

She got to her feet and began to undress. She kicked off her shoes and placed them side by side at the foot of the narrow bed. She pulled her sweater up over her head, folded it neatly and placed it on the bed. She opened and unzipped her skirt, stepped out of it, folded it and put it beside the sweater. She was now wearing only a bra and panties.

She took off the bra. Her breasts were firm and full. In time, she thought, they would swell with milk. She closed her eyes for just the shortest moment and remembered the touch of Ronnie's hands upon her breasts, and something turned over inside her and she caught her breath.

She placed the bra upon the bed.

She took off her panties and folded her hands over her flat stomach. Flat now, she thought, but given time it would grow round, and she would feel life within it . . .

She stopped thinking those thoughts.

For a moment she stood straight and tall, and at that moment she was quite lovely. A beautiful body, tall and straight and well put together, the skin smooth and flawless, the carriage erect.

Then she took hold of the razor blade.

She made a tiny cut on her left wrist and whispered, "Oh, I am afraid," and she made another try and stopped herself thinking *Can I do it? Can I?* She tried again, another small cut, and she watched blood ooze very slowly from the three tiny cuts on her left wrist, and she thought *Oh, God help me* and slashed open the veins in her left wrist and transferred the blade from one hand to the other and slashed again, quickly and unwaveringly, through the vein in her right wrist.

The razor blade dropped slowly to the floor, bounced once and was still. She sat on the edge of the bed and stared at her wrists. The blood flowed evenly. Now I get tired, she thought and then I weaken and then it all stops. I am all that is left, alone and lost and weary, and soon I will be gone like everything and everyone, the building and Mommy and Daddy and Ted and Ronnie and—

Oh my God oh my God!

When she did move, after so short a time that seemed like so long a time, when she got to her feet and began to scream, when she lurched for the door, shrieking, she was already beginning to weaken. She got to the door and got it open and stood crying out in the hallway, gripping one wrist with the opposite hand while the unheld wrist went on bleeding freely. There were noises in the building, sounds of human movement, and there was a man coming toward her. His face swam in and out of focus.

She said, "Oh, Ronnie, you're back, you'll save me."

She said, "Help me, I'm dying."

She said, "I'm sorry."

And then, as the man reached her, her legs gave way and she fell forward and the darkness came in like fog.

Chapter 2

There was a long stretch of gray and black, an endless time of dreaming and waking and sleeping. The dreams were bad ones, and it was as well that she did not remember them. The periods of consciousness were hazy at best and did not stay with her long.

Until finally she opened her eyes and saw a man in white standing by the side of her bed looking down at her. He was scowling. She tried to change position on the bed but couldn't. Her feet were tied to the foot of the bed.

He said, "Well, you lost the baby, Karen."

She looked at him.

"Shock and loss of blood turned the trick. Lost the baby, and damn near lost yourself in the bargain. There must be an easier way to induce abortion than by slashing your wrists. But I suppose you were trying to kill more than the baby, weren't you?"

"I—"

"Do you know what day it is? October twenty-seventh. You attempted suicide on—" He looked at her chart "—the 19th of September. You've been here about six weeks Does that surprise you?"

It did.

"We almost lost you. The man who found you outside your room managed to stop the bleeding but by that time you had already lost a lot of blood. You had transfusions. Then we realized you were pregnant and you lost the kid and hemorrhaged and almost died all over again. Shock. How do you feel now?"

"I don't know."

He nodded thoughtfully "You'll have to stay here a few days. When people try to kill themselves they don't realize what a headache they're giving the rest of the world. You can't just go ahead and kill yourself when you feel like it. Not in a civilized country. It's against the law. I'm not sure of the wisdom of the law, to tell you the truth. Sometimes I think a person should have the right to go to hell whatever way he wants to. But this country isn't geared that way. People have to go on living whether they want to or not. Are you sorry to be alive, Karen?"

She wasn't, and she said as much. Her head felt very light. She thought that she was going to be sick, but this didn't happen. She had the feeling that she ought to be thanking this doctor but she didn't know just how to go about it.

"Karen? I have to ask you some questions. You can lie to me if you feel like it. It doesn't much matter."

"I—"

"You killed yourself because you were pregnant? Tried to kill yourself, I mean. Is that right?"

"I suppose so."

"You were depressed about it?"

"Yes."

"You're not married, of course."

She shook her head.

"Know who the father is? The man who would have been the father if you had left him something to be the father of?"

She winced at the words. It was beginning to soak in—she had had life within her, and she had destroyed that life by trying to kill herself. She was alive but the baby was not.

"I know," she said.

"He wouldn't marry you?"

"No." She swallowed. "He left," she said.

"You told him you were pregnant and he ran out on you? Sounds like a sweet guy. Tell me, Karen, what do you think you'll be doing after we let you out of here?"

He went on asking her questions and she answered them briefly without giving them much thought. After awhile he went away and left her alone. A nurse came in later on with a tray and asked her how she was feeling. She ate lunch, had her temperature and blood pressure taken, took a nap. She stayed at the hospital for four days and answered a great many questions asked by several different doctors. What would she do when she left? Where would she live? Would she get a job? Where? Doing what? She had a college degree, she knew how to type, she had had a job in an office until one day she had simply failed to come in, and she would get another job with no trouble. Money? There was some in the bank, some she had forgotten somehow in the middle of everything. How much? A few hundred dollars, she wasn't sure exactly how much. Her clothes and bankbook and everything else were in that room on West 74th Street, the room where she had been living, the room where she had lived with Ronnie. She would find another room, and another job, and everything would work itself out.

They spent four days keeping her under observation and letting her rest. At first she was not at all impatient to leave the hospital. She was strong enough, completely recovered, but she had no place to go and nothing to do, really, and so she was happy enough to stay where she was. In the hospital there was a room for her and a bed for her, and they brought food to her and told her when to wake up and when to sleep. The security was as comfortable as a warm blanket. But by the fourth day it began to get on her nerves. She still had no real plans but she knew that it was time for her to go, time to leave, time to get started doing something.

They seemed to know it, too. In mid-afternoon of the fourth day of consciousness they told her it was time to go. She signed herself out and left.

For a week she went through motions without giving herself time to do any thinking. She went to her old room and collected her clothing and books from the landlady. She did not want to live there any more. There were too many memories in the room and they were all wrong ones. She picked up a copy of the *Times* and looked at the listings of furnished rooms. She wanted a neighborhood which was somewhat familiar but not one where she had lived before. The West Seventies were as full of memories as the room she was giving up. Brooklyn and the Bronx were too far away. She would be living in Manhattan and she wanted to live reasonably close to her job. Greenwich Village would have been ideal, but the few rooms listed were too expensive.

She took the first room she looked at, a small but comfortable room in a brownstone rooming house on East Nineteenth Street near Irving Place. The rent was twelve dollars a week, and the man who rented it to her told her she could heat things up on a hot plate if she wanted.

She settled herself down, applied for half a dozen jobs, drank a great many cups of coffee, smoked innumerable cigarettes, took long quiet walks through her new neighborhood. She decided that she liked it. The residential parts were quiet and clean, the people in the area mostly widows with insurance money and older couples living on pensions. There were not many children. Some students, a handful of young married couples.

On a Friday, six days after she signed herself out of the hospital, she went to an office on Fourth Avenue to apply for a job. The office was hardly larger than the room she lived in, and the man in the office was a fifty-year-old theatrical booking agent with sparse hair, a facial tic, and a gravel voice. He sat behind a desk covered with papers and photos. The walls were plastered with inscribed photographs of girls Karen did not recognize.

"Easy job," the agent told her. "First of the month I get out of here and into a better office. More space, you know what I mean? One room like what you see here, except bigger, and there's an anteroom in front for a receptionist. That's you. You answer the phone, you place calls for me, you look pretty." He furrowed his forehead. "That's the main thing, I'll tell you now. Looking pretty and having a pretty voice on the phone. That's why I wanted you to call first, so I could see how you sound on the phone. Too many of the girls who would go for a cushy job like this, they chew gum all the time or they're ugly as pigs or they got a voice that's pure Bronx. Doesn't give an office a feeling of class, y'unnerstand?"

She nodded uncertainly.

"What it is, see, is there's not much real work. Twenty years I sit behind a desk, I answer the phone myself, I make calls myself. All right, it works fine that way. A cinch. That's what this business is— knowing who to call and knowing the person and what to say to him and how much to ask. Your office is your hat, that way, that type of scene. The clients I represent, it's like you're selling meat in a meat market. But I figure a little class doesn't hurt. Twenty years in this business and if you make it, well, you begin to attract a higher type of client, or some of your clients begin to break through and some of them stay with you instead of jumping to William Morris. It happens one or two of them have a feeling of loyalty. You want the job?"

She blinked at him.

"Yes? No?"

"Yes," she said.

"Sixty a week?"

She would have agreed readily except that she was too dazzled by the endless flow of words to say anything at all. The hesitation was not a bad idea. The agent misinterpreted it.

"So let's say seventy," he said. "Sixty would be better for me. I won't kid you, that extra ten is money. But if I have a girl working for me I want her happy where she is, you know? She should have enough dough so she won't spend her lunch hours looking for another job. Seventy?"

"That's fine," she said.

"You could start now only there's no place to put you, not in this place. First of the month we move up to Third Avenue and Forty-third. It's a better location than this. This they call Park Avenue

South now, but anybody with a head knows it's still Fourth Avenue. And Fifth is better."

There was more but she just nodded politely and half-listened until he stopped to answer a phone and mutter something unintelligible into it. When he finished he asked her if there were any questions, and she said that there weren't. He told her he would see her the first of the month at the new office. She thanked him and left.

So she had a job. Later that afternoon she sat in her own room drinking a cup of instant coffee and smoking a cigarette and thinking about it. The agent's name was Leon Gordon, and his office was called LeGo Associates, and she was working for him. The pay was not too bad, either. She had been earning seventy-five dollars a week on her last job, and this was less than that, but in time she might be able to get a raise.

And she was just as glad that she had some free time before the job began. She could afford it—the money from her savings account was more than enough to sustain her until the job started. She had been busy for a week, job-hunting, getting settled. Now a few weeks of inertia were welcome.

She had almost killed herself.

This was rather hard to believe. So much had happened, all so strange and out of character. She had become pregnant. Ronnie had left her. She had gone slightly crazy, and she had wound up bleeding very nearly to death in a foul little room somewhere on the Lower East Side.

Hard to believe, and quite terrifying. She had to straighten herself out, had to work out a little pattern for living. The routine of work would be valuable to her, but in the meanwhile a little time to herself would be very good for her.

Ronnie.

His name leaped at her without warning, and she felt herself stiffen at once with fear and horror. She stood up and walked to her window and held onto the windowsill to steady herself. He had seduced her, he was the first and only man to do that, and she had fallen in love with him, so completely in love with him. She conceived his child and he left her and she tried to kill herself and killed his child—and her child as well.

Where was he now? In California, she guessed. He had said something to that effect on the awful night when he left her. And he had mentioned California before. He wanted to be an actor, and he had not been able to get anywhere in New York, so now he would try his luck in Hollywood.

She prayed that she would never see him again. She had loved him so much, and now all she had in love's place was cold and uncompromising hate. She had loved him and he took her love and threw it in her face. She had loved him, and had damn near died of it.

No more.

Never again, she told herself. Not with Ronnie, not with anyone. A man's love could only be bad for a woman. A man was a two-faced, a worrisome thing who—no, that was from a song, some kind of song that she could not quite remember. But true, very true. Men used you and when they were done they left you with your heart in pieces or else they stayed with you, and you wound up with nothing but a ratty apartment surrounded by children and dirty dishes and unpayable bills and a man out of work, wound up trapped by a man and drowning in marriage.

Oh no, never again. No more loving, no more cutting yourself into bite-sized pieces for a man who would use you up and discard you when he was done with you. No more of that. Not now, not later, not ever. Never, never.

Her room felt suddenly like a cage. She grabbed up her purse and put on her coat and bolted. Outside she walked to Gramercy Park and stood outside the heavy iron gate. The park was a private one, and only the tenants in certain buildings had the right to enter it. There was something horrible about this, she decided. A park ought to belong to whoever wanted to sit in it. It wasn't right to fence off a rare chunk of trees and greenness and make them off-limits to anyone who lacked a key. But that was the way it was. She had no key, and she could not go inside.

She smoked a cigarette. In a way, she knew, she was a very lucky young woman. She knew this herself, and one of the doctors at the hospital had taken great pains to reinforce the fact. She was very fortunate. She had done a stupid thing with a stupid razor blade, and she would always carry scars on her wrists to remind her of her stupidity. She had done something stupid but now she had a second chance. She was alive. With care, she could build a new life for herself. She could grab hold of this second shot at life and make something good out of it.

The next day, Saturday, she slept late. She had brunch around the corner at a luncheonette and wandered around the neighborhood and went to a movie, an Italian film that proved its artistic integrity and high purpose by drifting in and out of focus. She ate dinner at an inexpensive Armenian restaurant on Eighteenth Street and went back to her room and read for awhile.

Sunday she spent most of the day reading the Sunday *Times*. There was a free concert of baroque chamber music in the Village, on Bedford Street. She went to it and got utterly lost in the music.

Afterward she had a little trouble falling asleep. There were bad dreams, and she wound up getting out of bed while it was still fairly dark outside.

Monday, Tuesday, Wednesday.

Wednesday evening, at dinner, she realized quite suddenly that she had somehow managed to go several days without speaking to a single person. Beyond the words necessary to order a meal or buy a newspaper, she had not spoken at all to anyone.

She did not know anyone. She might have called someone on the phone but there was no one to call. The friends from her last job were office friends—you chatted gaily with them from nine to five and then forgot them completely. The friends from her life on West 74th Street were Ronnie's friends more than her own. She would not have seen them for anything.

She felt terribly alone, violently alone. She went to her room and thought how alone she was, tried to read a book but could not keep track of the words on the pages. She put the book down and stretched out on the narrow bed and buried her face in the pillow. All at once she was crying. The tears flowed like a river. She lay very still on her bed and cried her eyes out.

There was nothing suicidal about her depression, nothing deep and bitter. She was a girl alone and she wanted someone to talk to and had no one, and she cried.

This would change, she tried to tell herself. Once the job started, once she began to meet people, all of this would change soon enough. She would meet a few girls, and some of them would be interesting people to talk with, and gradually she would become someone's friend. All she needed was a friend. Movies and concerts were more fun if you went with someone than if you crept alone to them.

A simple thing like a walk around the block meant more if you had company. Every aspect of your life had more meaning if there was another person on earth who could react to it.

In a way, she realized, it was loneliness that had prepared her for Ronnie. With her mother dead and Ted in the army she had been terribly alone. Ronnie had been such fine company at first, so good to be with. The sharing, the closeness—that had been the force that made love so wonderful for her. The rest of it, the bed part, it all came from the loneliness.

She would not make that mistake again. There was a way to avoid loneliness without making a fool out of yourself for a man. There had to be a way. A girl could stay single without turning into a lonely friendless caricature of spinsterhood. There would be a way, and she would find it.

Two days later, on Friday, she saw the new girl for the first time. She had gone down to the front hall to check her mail, not that she ever expected any mail. There was none, of course, but in the hallway she had seen the girl come in carrying a small suitcase. A cab driver followed her with more baggage in tow.

The girl was a striking blonde, tall, full-formed, with long hair that fell loose to her shoulders. She looked about twenty-four or twenty-five. Karen smiled at her, and the girl smiled back quickly, and then she was on her way up the stairs.

She thought of the girl later that day. She saw her from her window the next morning. The blonde girl was on her way to the corner mailbox with a letter in hand. It would be so good to have a friend in the building, she thought. And she smiled wryly and thought that it would be good to have a friend anywhere.

But how did you begin? Probably the blonde girl was not looking for friends. Probably the blonde girl had friends all over the city and was perfectly happy as she was. Probably the blonde girl was engaged, and after a few months on East Nineteenth Street she would marry some rising junior executive and move out to Long Island to make babies and gain weight.

Sunday she met the blonde girl and spoke to her for the first time. She was on her way back from the newsstand with her *Times* in tow, and the blonde girl was headed for the luncheonette. They smiled at each other, and the blonde girl said, "I guess we're neighbors. You live at one-oh-five, don't you?"

"Yes. You just moved in?"

"Friday. I thought you were the girl I saw in the hallway. But I always get sort of dizzy when I move into a new place. It's confusing, trying to keep track of your luggage and to guess what you forgot to pack. Have you been here long?"

"Less than three weeks."

"Do you like it? My room's tiny but it seems comfortable so far. I'm not used to just a room, actually. I was sharing an apartment with another girl, but when she moved out I couldn't afford to stay there by myself. My name is Rae, by the way. Short for Rachel, which is a pretty terrible name. Rae Cooper."

"I'm Karen Winslow."

"My pleasure." Rae smiled suddenly. "I'm not going to hold you up. I'll see you around the dormitory, neighbor."

Twice that afternoon she was on the point of finding the blonde's room and going to it. Once she forced her attention back to the crossword puzzle and another time she took a walk around the block instead. Rae had been very friendly and she couldn't help hoping it might turn into a real friendship, but she was afraid to be pushy about it. That would not be good at all.

In a way, she had trouble understanding her own nervousness. She was twenty-two years old, old enough to carry on a conversation with another girl without getting shaky in the knees. Maybe it was just that she was so very much alone, she thought, or that she had built up this need for a friend in her mind to the point where it made her shaky.

Whatever it was, she was sure it would work itself out. She and Rae were just two girls who happened to live in the same building. With any luck at all they would get to know one another. And the big glaring gap in her life would start to fill itself a little.

When the knock came at her door a few minutes after six, she was not expecting it. She almost jumped.

"It's me," she heard Rae say. "Busy?"

She opened the door. Rae was standing there, dressed in a sweater that was tight on her large breasts and a skirt that clung to her hips. She had a coat over one arm.

"If I'm interrupting anything," she said, "just tell me and I'll go away."

"Oh, I was just sitting around."

"Did you have dinner yet?"

"No, not yet."

"Any plans? A big evening with some man or anything? Because if you haven't got anything lined up, I thought we could have dinner together. Unless you're tied up . . ."

"I'm not."

"Good. I hate eating alone and I've been doing nothing else lately. There's a Chinese restaurant a few blocks from here that's not half bad. Do you like Chinese food?"

"Yes, very much."

"Throw a coat on," Rae said. "If you feel like it, that is. I'm starving, myself and I'm sick of sitting around staring at the walls. I'm dying for company, Karen."

Chapter 3

The Chinese restaurant was pleasant enough but she hardly noticed it. She was too excited by Rae's company to pay much attention to her surroundings or the food she ate. It seemed as if she couldn't stop talking, as though everything Rae said to her was the most fascinating thing she had ever heard. *How lonely I've been,* she thought. *How very lonely I've been.*

She talked about her job and how impatient she was to get started with it. "You'd better watch yourself," Rae said. "Some of those Broadway types are pretty quick at chasing a girl around a desk."

She grinned at the image of Mr. Gordon chasing anyone anywhere. "I don't think my boss is the type."

"You can never tell, Karen. Especially with a pretty girl like you."

"He won't even notice me."

"Don't bet on it."

"Now with all the showgirls he handles."

"Handles?" Rae said archly. They both laughed. "Of course," the blonde girl went on, "some girls like to be chased. And to be caught."

"Not me."

"No?"

She lowered her eyes, stared at her cup of green tea. "I'm not very interested in men," she said.

"Oh?"

"There was . . . oh, I don't know. Private problems, I guess. Now here I'm getting all moody, and that's a terrible thing."

"Feel like talking about it, Karen?"

"I don't think so."

"All right."

"Just that I don't think I'll be dating much. I'm not really interested, I guess. Once burned and twice shy, or something like that. I'll leave it to you to be the Betty Coed of Nineteenth Street."

"Not me, I'm afraid."

"You're not a man-hater too, are you?"

Rae had a funny look in her eyes. She started to say something, then stopped and changed her mind. "Some other time," she said.

"Sure."

Rae changed the subject. She started to talk now about her own work, which Karen found quite fascinating. Rae had taken a commercial art course in college and had worked for a year in an uptown studio. Now she was freelancing, doing occasional jobs as an illustrator of juvenile books.

"You don't get rich that way," she said, "but I like the work, and the life that goes with it. It used to kill me to drag myself out of bed early every morning and hop onto the subway. This way I set my own hours and take things easy. And I like the work."

"Have you had many books published with your illustrations?"

"A few."

"I'd love to see them."

"You won't have to twist my arm. I've got a few around the room.

I'll show them to you later, if you're interested." She lit a cigarette. "Say, do you have room to work in your place? I don't know how your room compares to mine in size—"

"About the same. Which means small."

"Oh."

"Do you work there?"

"I haven't tried yet, actually. I've just moved in, and I'm not in the middle of anything at the moment. I have an assignment but there's no rush at all on it and I can stall for a week or so. I've thought about it, though, and it may be tricky. The room isn't exactly spacious and the lighting isn't very good at all. I don't need a perfect north light. God knows I'm no great artiste, but the light ought to be fairly decent and there should be more space. When you live where you work you need more space just to keep from going off your nut, whatever kind of work it is that you do."

"Won't that be a problem?"

"It might."

"Then . . ."

"You see, I just took this room on a temporary basis, Karen. Sooner or later I'll run into somebody who feels like sharing a place, and then I'll have a decent apartment. So even if I'm cramped for awhile it won't matter."

Maybe they could share an apartment, she thought suddenly. She almost said something before she realized how foolish it would sound. After all, she and Rae barely knew each other. You had to know someone pretty well before the two of you were ready to set up housekeeping together.

Still, it was something for her to think about. How insecure you're getting, she told herself. So hungry for a friend that you're ready to sign a lease after an hour of conversation. It was crazy, but at the same time she couldn't dodge the feeling that she and Rae were going to be a great deal more than just casual friends. She didn't know why this was, but the feeling persisted.

They settled the check, left the restaurant and headed back toward their building. The air had a chill to it. They walked quickly.

Maybe it was the wine.

They were in Rae's room, a little cubicle very much like Karen's room except that it was a flight up and its window fronted on an air shaft instead of the street. She had admired three books Rae had illustrated, one about a squirrel who buried a nut and couldn't find it, one about a small boy playing with boats, and one with illustrations of different breeds of cats. Then Rae suggested cracking a bottle of wine, and now they were sitting around sipping wine, she on a chair and Rae on the bed, and her head felt wondrously light and she thought that she was probably a little bit drunk.

She hadn't planned on talking about Ronnie. The subject came up of its own accord, and the wine probably loosened her tongue, and once she got started it was easier to go on than to stop. Like Macbeth, perhaps, so far steeped in blood that it was easier to go on than to turn back. A slightly mangled quotation, she thought, but one that would do for the time being.

Rae turned the talk in that direction. "Just a pair of old maids," she said. "We ought to live on Gramercy Park and keep a cat. On a nice night like this we should both be out with a couple of men, Karen."

"Not me."

"You sure make it sound bitter, don't you?"

"I've been feeling bitter."

"About men?"

"Uh-huh."

"Oh?"

"I'll show you something," she said. She leaned forward in her chair and held out her left hand palm up. Rae's eyes fastened on the scars on her wrist.

"I saw that," Rae said. "How—"

"The other wrist is the same way. I used a razor blade."

"Oh God."

"Uh-huh." She started to take a small sip of her wine and wound up draining the glass. Rae filled it from the bottle. "It's a long story," she said. "An ugly one."

"Tell me."

Once she got started, the words came surprisingly easily. She had been trying to avoid thinking about the whole affair with Ronnie, the beginning and the middle and the ending, all of it. But you couldn't force yourself to forget something like that. You could only push it back where it lay waiting to spring out all at once. It sprang out now in a rush of words, and she talked non-stop, running on and on like an endless tape recording, babbling and sputtering and spilling out words.

It was good for her. She realized as much while she talked. It was good to tell about it, good to let it out of her system. And the simple act of talking about it seemed to draw her closer to the blonde girl on the bed. She stopped from time to time for a sip of wine, and she thought from time to time how odd and wonderful it was that she had found someone to whom she could talk this way. It was no good to keep everything inside you. If she had had a really good friend right after the break-up with Ronnie, maybe she could have unwound a little instead of going on to tense up more and more and finally making a crazy try at suicide. She had had no one, and things had grown worse instead of better.

"Anyhow," she said finally, "I lived through it."

"You poor kid. God what a mess."

"I've been trying to tell myself that all men aren't as bad as he was. Maybe someday I'll be able to believe it, but for the time being I'm not running around looking for a man."

"They're all bad, Karen."

"Are they?"

"Most of them are worse. At least your guy turned out honest. He didn't try to con you forever. He showed himself the way he was. Other men just drag you along endlessly. They use you and they enjoy themselves and that's all there is to it. I'll tell you something— you're a damn sight better off this way."

"Am I?"

"I think so. You lived through it. Oh, you've picked up a couple of scars, some on the outside and some on the inside. But you've learned a thing or two."

"I guess I have."

She thought that she seemed to be slurring her words slightly. Take it easy on the wine, she told herself. But Rae filled her glass again, and the wine was very smooth and very dry, and she did feel good, after all, and what was the harm in sipping it slowly like this?

She wasn't much used to wine. When she and Ronnie sat drinking with Ronnie's friends they usually had beer, or sometimes mixed drinks. The wine was no stronger than some things she had had, but she wasn't quite used to it. This seemed to make a difference. It was nice, though. It gave her a good feeling, a warm feeling. Outside it had started to rain, and she could imagine what it was like outside, the air cold, a wind lashing icy rain about. This made the warmth and lazy comfort of the room all the more important.

"Karen? I'm glad you could talk about it."

"About what?"

"About what happened to you. About that man."

All about Ronnie, she thought. That was a song title. Chris Connor sang it. "All About Ronnie"—the melody hummed in her head, lazy and crystal cool.

"I feel very close to you now, Karen. It's as though we've known each other for such a long time."

"I feel the same way."

"Sit next to me."

She got up from the chair, and moved to the bed. She sat beside Rae and Rae filled their glasses again. They drank and she felt dizzy but not unpleasantly dizzy, and it was as though she could actually feel the warmth of the girl sitting beside her, and . . .

Rae was kissing her before she was aware of what was going on. Rae had turned toward her, and Rae's arms were around her and the clean sweet girl-smell of Rae was everywhere, and Rae's lips—so red, so full—were on her own lips, and she could feel the gentle pressure of Rae's body against her own yielding flesh, and Rae was kissing her and she did not know what was happening.

The wine, the warmth, the wind outside.

Rae's voice, a whisper in her hair. "Oh, sweet, sweet, sweet Karen.

Poor girl, poor lost girl. We're together now. You and I, together, and everything will be all right, baby, poor baby."

Her heart was beating faster and she felt blood pulsing in a vein on her temple. She did not understand. Rae kissed her again and she submitted to the kiss, receiving it passionlessly. Rae kissed her a third time, and something happened deep inside her and she felt her own arms going around Rae and her lips opening to accept the kiss.

Rae's tongue slipped between Karen's lips, and the kiss grew and spread, and she tasted Rae's mouth all wine-sweet and passion-warm, and all of the wine caught up with her and she was lost, caught up in something she did not understand and too drunk with wine and with Rae to stop long enough to figure it out.

She could neither think nor act. She could do nothing but go along with whatever Rae began, could do nothing but receive whatever Rae bestowed.

The wine, the warmth, the wind outside.

Rae went on kissing her, and all at once Rae's hands were all over her, everywhere, reaching to hold her breasts and press them and bring them awake to passion. She gasped as Rae touched her breasts. She did not understand this. This was the sort of thing a man would do to you, and she was afraid of a man doing this, but Rae was not a man, and it did not make sense to her.

And it was so different from the embrace of a man. Slowly, gently, Rae began to undress her. Slowly, gently. Rae guided her so that she fell back tenderly upon the bed, and Rae removed the last of her clothing, and Rae turned out all of the lights but one small lamp on the dresser, and Karen watched in the soft hazy glow of the lamplight as Rae took off all of her own clothing as well.

Rae was beautiful. Rae's breasts were large, larger than her own, and they were perfectly formed and shaped. Rae was a big girl but there was not an ounce of fat on her frame, just smooth sweet girl-flesh. Rae was next to her, on the bed with her, and Rae kissed her again, a long kiss, and this time their bare bodies met and pressed close, and the effect was twice as intoxicating as the wine had been, twice as dizzying, twice as maddening in its intensity.

She had never felt this way. Nothing had ever been like this, and she did not understand it and did not attempt to understand it. She felt the exquisite sensation of Rae's bare breasts against her own bare breasts, the pressure, the warmth, and she knew only that she needed this warmth, that it was heavenly and wonderful and good for her. Rae's body was a warm sweet cave, and she could crawl into it and surrender herself to it and be safe within it.

So different from a man. With Ronnie it had always been fast and urgent, a swift desperate plunge after pleasure which was pleasure for him more than pleasure for her. A handful of preliminary caresses tossed at her as a peace offering, and then he invaded her. And then it was over and she was shaky and he was ready for nothing but sleep and snoring.

So very different, as night from day, as dark from night. Rae played upon her warm sweet body as a virtuoso violinist upon his instrument, drawing from it notes and tones unlike anything the violin had ever emitted before. Rae touched her and kissed her and her flesh sang.

Her breasts. Rae's hands cupped her breasts and whispered to them, the tips of Rae's fingers so firm and yet so gentle on her taut flesh, teasing until her nipples stiffened with yearning, gentle, gentle, tender and gentle, and her body crazy from the love but her mind nevertheless strangely calm.

It was all so strange. There was none of that awful urgency, no need to hurry, no need to rush. There was just a beautiful glow of warmth that spread and spread at its own pace, with sensation piling on top of sensation and her head swimming and the winds of love roaring in her ears.

Her breasts and Rae's hands on her breasts, and Rae's mouth on her mouth. And then, ever so gradually, Rae moving upon her, moving slowly, and Rae's mouth leaving her mouth and a rain of kisses all over her face, on her cheeks, on the tip of her pointed chin, over her throat and shoulders.

Her breasts and Rae kissing her breasts, with lips so soft and gentle. Rae's tongue bathing the soft skin on the undersides of her breasts like the summer rain on a flowerbed, gentle, soft, tender, pitching her passion inexorably higher.

The cool sweet feel of Rae's cheek on the flat of Karen's waist.

The welcome probing of Rae's hands on Karen's legs.

There was a moment, brief but definite, when an awful clarity came to it all. There was a moment when she saw at once that something very strange was happening, something darkly shadowed, something forbidden. There was that moment, filled with fear, shaky, the moment, perhaps, of truth.

And the moment passed. The moment came and went, and resistance never entered the picture and surrender remained the sole theme, surrender, yielding, acceptance. There was Rae, bestowing a caress so intimate, so perfect, so tender, so wonderful, and there was Karen, soaring higher than she had ever soared before, caught up entirely in passion, floating on wings of shadowy love.

The wine, the warmth, the wind outside. And Rae, and Rae's delicious love.

Chapter 4

Morning. Cold, grey, dreadful. Rain fell steadily and soundlessly, a thin and washed-out rain that dropped cheerlessly through dead still air. She sat, unmindful of the rain, on a wet bench in Gramercy Park. She had been walking and she had reached the park gate just as a man was leaving. He held the gate open for her without questioning her right to enter, and she walked in and found her bench. The gates were once again locked, and one could not leave without a key. Sooner or later, she knew, someone would come to permit her to leave. Until then she was quite content to sit on her bench and be washed by the powdery rain.

Morning. Wine leaves a wicked residue in the body and the spirit. No headache, no dizziness, no sharp little pains. Just a general malaise, an overall combination of uneasiness and discontent. An upset stomach, a bad dose of heartburn, and unquenchable thirst—these were the aftereffects she felt.

Above and beyond them, superimposed upon them, was an overwhelming devastating sense of sin.

What had she done? What had she permitted? What, heaven help her, had she so dreadfully *enjoyed?*

She did not want to think about it. And, inevitably, she could think of nothing else. The impossible memory of what she had done and what had been done to her blanketed everything. She sat on the bench, fighting the sense of sin and trying to conjure up a satisfactory vision of her personal self. She was trapped, suffocating, stomach turning over and heart on fire, and she could not even think straight.

Words and phrases, creatures of memory, rushed at her like men with drawn bayonets. They came bereft of punctuation, devoid of intonation, racing though her mind in a river.

Karen Karen darling I love you it's all right it's all right believe me don't you understand you never did this before did you did you oh it's good darling believe me it's good I swear it Karen Karen look at me darling it's not wrong it's not wrong nothing is wrong at all not when two people love each other Karen men are no good for people like us you see that don't you it's true Karen darling I knew it the day I saw you do you believe that and I plotted this I admit it and if you want to think I'm a devil for doing it you may and I love you and need you Karen I've been with men and I know they're no good and a woman has to love and be loved it's a necessity Karen don't look at me like that Karen oh darling don't you see I couldn't help myself I couldn't I loved you from the minute I saw you Karen believe me it's true . . .

Rain descending, falling steadily. A slight breeze whipping the rain along. Words, ribbons of words, all unwinding.

Karen where are you going Karen don't leave now Karen stay with me please you have to let me explain God there are so many things I have to tell you Karen please wait oh Karen I'm sorry I'm so sorry . . .

Flight. Down hall, down stairs. Her own room, her door slammed abruptly shut, as securely shut as a closed coffin lid. The lock turned, the room embracing her like a grave.

Let me in Karen you have to let me in you have to let me talk to you oh God how could I let this happen how could I be so stupid Karen you know what we did you know it was good Karen it was good for both of us and you have to admit it Karen I'm sorry forgive me please let me in Karen just say that you forgive me and I'll go away and leave you alone Karen say that much or I'll stay here all night I swear it just give me that much darling oh Karen I'm sorry Karen I'm going now and I'm sorry I mean it it's the truth I really am sorry Karen . . .

Footsteps trailing down the hallway and disappearing. And a long time of sitting and staring and wanting to weep. No tears came. At last she got out of her clothes and into her bed and the wine worked quickly and carried her off to sleep. But there was morning, inevitably, and now she sat in Gramercy Park, locked inside, letting the rain wash her and knowing that nothing, not even the rain, would be enough to rinse her clean again.

Damp and chilled, feverish, she left the park somewhere in the early afternoon and found her way back to her room. The day seemed to last forever but finally drew to a close. She went to sleep around midnight, tired and drawn, without having seen Rae at all that day. She got into bed expecting to toss and turn for hours and certain that bad dreams would wake her all through the night. She surprised herself. Sleep came quickly, and morning came as quickly and if there were any dreams they were forgotten entirely when she awoke.

She left her apartment early in the day. The sun was bright, the air warm and fresh. She rode a bus to 42nd Street and went to a movie. She left after the first show ended and walked to a cafeteria. She sat for several hours drinking coffee and smoking cigarettes. No one talked to her, no one bothered her. The coffee sharpened the edge of thought. Her mind worked swiftly.

Calmly and soberly and dispassionately she reviewed everything she knew of lesbians. The initial pit of black reaction had evaporated with yesterday's raindrops. Now she tried to determine what she thought and what she felt.

She had never given lesbians much thought, she realized. There had been girls whom she had recognized as homosexual, girls she had heard that kind of talk about, but she had never known one of them well, had never had a lesbian for a friend. She had known two male homosexuals, both of them members of the uptown world she and Ronnie had inhabited. The area—the West Seventies—was glutted with them. Gay jokes had been a standard item in her social circle at the time.

Had she ever had strong feelings one way or the other? Not that she remembered. One of the fellows—funny, but she couldn't recall his name—had been very nice to her, always anxious to talk to her while most of the others in that group were Ronnie's friends and accepted her only because she was living with him. Phillip, that was his name, had been a friend, and the fact that he was a homosexual had never entered into their relationship. It was simply what he was; had he been an Italian, or a salesman, or a bald-headed man, it would have meant as much to her.

Ronnie had joked about it. *At least don't have to* worry *about Phillie beating my time with you. You just haven't got what he's looking for, kid. You're not his type . . .*

And on the night when she told him of her pregnancy, and he gave her a verbal slap with *How do I know it's mine, kid?* Biting back tears, she asked who he thought might have fathered the child. *For all I know it's Phillie-Boy's,* he had said, and his harsh laughter tore her to little pieces.

She put out a cigarette in an ashtray and finished her coffee. She carried the cup to the counter and brought back a fresh one and lit another cigarette while she waited for the coffee to cool to a drink-able temperature. She remembered, rationally now, her feelings af-ter Rae had made love to her. The delicious glow had endured for a moment, and then it was gone in a rush and the agony and sinful-ness and loathing took its place.

Why?

She could not answer this question satisfactorily. It did not make sense for her to react so blindly. Something had happened between them, something which she might easily have written off as little more than an unpredictable side-effect of too much wine and an overdose of the lonelies. She could have shrugged off the whole expe-rience or she could have cast Rae as the seductive ogre and rational-ized her own part in the proceedings.

Yet she had done none of these things. She had hated herself at least as much as she had hated the blonde girl, and she had let herself drift around in a fog for a whole day, sitting in the rain and running a strong risk of catching pneumonia or being hauled off to Bellevue as a catatonic. And out of what? Out of a monumental fear-hate for homosexuality? Why?

Because you liked it, Karen.

She tapped a cigarette on the back of one hand, so calm now, so mentally efficient. Because she liked it? Was that the explanation?

Two cigarettes and three cups of black coffee later, she knew more about herself than she had ever known before. She turned both hands palm-up and looked at her wrists, at the white lines upon them, the thin ones where she had made her first attempts, the thicker deeper ones that had nearly snuffed her out. The doctor had told her she would carry those scars for a long time. Perhaps forever. And she looked at them now and thought of the invisible scars that everyone carried and that she would always possess. Some scar tissue never went away. It might heal, it might grow stronger than the original flesh, but it was scarred and it remained that way.

She knew. Oh, she knew.

⤳•⤲

For two days she let the world alone and the world in turn ignored her. The job would start soon. She had called Leon Gordon once to make sure that everything was in order, and the agent told her she could report to work Monday morning. "Got a jump on the lease, kid," he explained. "The bum who was in here moved out in a hurry owing money to half the town, so you can start first of the week. And take care of that voice. You gotta keep sounding refined."

Twice she had seen Rachel Cooper. Once from her window. She was sitting at the window, just sitting and thinking, and she saw the blonde girl emerge from their building and the wind whipping the long coat tight against her legs, the wind tossing the golden hair. A cab pulled up and Rae opened the door and got inside, and the door closed and the cab pulled away and was gone.

Another time they passed in the building's entranceway. Neither of them spoke. Karen had felt the rush of blood to her face. Her hands trembled like leaves in a windstorm. And for a moment Rae seemed on the verge of speaking, as if groping for a phrase, for the right words. They passed in silence.

One night she heard footsteps in the corridor. The steps halted at her door, and she waited for the knock but no knock came. There was a long moment of silence, and she ached to say something, anything, and then at last the footsteps resumed and Rae walked past her closed door without knocking.

Rae could have knocked. Or she could have called out, inviting the knock. But they had both waited.

In bed, waiting for sleep to come, she decided that she was glad the blonde girl had made no move. Rae had to desire her—this was important—but still she did not want to be pushed into anything, neither pushed nor pulled. She thought of this and smiled at the darkness and slept.

There were some thoughts to think about, so many thoughts to examine, so many feelings to mull over and attune to. One had to take time, she thought, because a mistake would be a disaster and she could not afford much more in the way of disaster. Yet there was not an eternity of time. Rae would not wait forever, and she herself could not wait forever.

At times, sitting over dinner, dreaming in her room over a book, she would feel a burst of longing and sit bolt upright, trying to define and appraise it. Sometimes she identified it as loneliness. When one is always silent, when one neither speaks nor is spoken to, when one carries on wordless conversations with one's self day in and day out, loneliness becomes a living thing to be contended with. She would react to a thought or a sight or anything at all and have no one with whom to share it. She would think so many things and have no opportunity to give them voice. She had never been the type to speak with strangers, to bandy small talk with shopkeepers. The thoughts and ideas stayed locked up inside and the loneliness grew like cancer.

Or there would be the sexual longings. These always came when she was not ready for them. Often in bed, late at night or early in the morning, when she was either awaiting sleep or drugged with it, there would be a tingling itch at the tips of her breasts or a quivering warmth at her loins, and her mind would begin to swirl away into dark fantasy before she knew quite what was happening. At times her hands would go to the source of discontent, embracing her breasts or groping for her loins, less to caress than to somehow reassure, and then she would redden with solitary embarrassment and force her mind and body away from lustfulness.

The loneliness and the longings all pointed the same way, toward a girl with golden hair and knowing hands and eager lips. It was just a question of time, and she knew this and knew it well. It was just a question of time, and, one Friday evening, one sweet evening, the time had come.

A dark night, thoroughly dark, moonless and starless. She sat a long time at the window, and she was still sitting there when a taxi stopped at the curb and Rae stepped out of it. Her heart gave a sudden almost painful throb, and her loins went instantly warm, and she knew it was time. For a horrid moment she was positive that she had waited too long, that there was someone with Rae. But no, the girl was alone.

She waited. There were footsteps on the stairs, and she heard them reach her floor and pass on upward. She waited, and she lit a cigarette and put it out after a single drag, and knew that it was time. In the bathroom she scrubbed her face clean and put on rouge and lipstick and a hint of eye-shadow. She checked the result and fussed with her hair and knew that she did not look at all pretty, that she was really a frightfully plain thing.

She trembled as she climbed the stairs. She walked softly across the floor to Rae's door, and she stood there for a few eternal seconds, and then she knocked, twice.

"Yes?"

"It's Karen," she said, She did not recognize her own voice. It sounded wholly unfamiliar, foreign.

The door opened. Eyes caught her own eyes. She stepped inside and drew a breath and pushed the door shut.

"I'm afraid I'm a silly person," she managed to say. "A stupid person, actually. There are too many things I just do not know. About myself, about . . . everything."

She caught her breath. Her head was whirling. "I'm sorry for being such a fool," she said. The words came a little easier now. "I want to be here. Now. With you."

Chapter 5

"Would you like to talk, Karen?"

"No."

"Can I get you anything to drink? I have a little Scotch left in the bottle, not very much, but—"

"No, thank you."

Tell me, Rae's eyes were saying. *Cue me in, let me know how you want me to play it. Fast or slow, hard or soft, let me know and we'll play it your way.*

"Just love me," she heard herself say. Her words surprised her, startled her. She took an involuntary step backward, surprised by what she had said, the boldness of her words, the stark nakedness of desire that underlay them. Was she then so very much in need? Was her desire that raw?

"Oh . . ."

There was a moment telescoped in time, a moment of hands reaching and flesh groping. She was transfixed, a bird hypnotized by a snake, a doe caught in a car's headlights at night. Until Rae caught her and held her and kissed her and tore the image forever out of focus.

Rae's lips on her own were feathers upon silk, hummingbird wings beating against the petals of a rose. Rae's hands held her shoulders, then moved down along her arms to her elbows, then caught her waist and passed around her back to draw her close. At first Karen's eyes were open, staring blindly at the closed eyes of the girl who was kissing her. Then, easily, her eyes fluttered shut and her heart beat audibly and her throat grew dust-dry, a deep burning aridness running all the way back from her mouth. Her knees melted. She thought she might fall, and she clutched Rae as if to keep herself from losing her balance entirely.

They kissed again. Now she gave herself up wholly to the kiss, her arms tightening around Rae, her lips parting of their own accord to accept the fullness of the kiss. She felt and was enormously conscious of the pressure of their bodies together, two fine and beautiful girl bodies, thighs pressed against thighs, breasts against breasts, mouths glued wetly together.

The fear and trembling died and melted away. The awful nameless anxiety drifted off. Rae's hand released their grip, Rae's lips withdrew, and Karen stood for a moment, eyes still shut, waiting. For an instant it was like waking at dawn, waking up from a good dream and hugging the pillow, reluctant to meet the day, reluctant to give up the warmth and sweetness of the dream.

Then she let go of it, when she opened her eyes, she saw Rae still standing in front of her, the ghost of a smile upon her lips.

"I'll turn out the lights."

"All right."

Rae crossed to the doorway, flicked the switch to turn off the bare lightbulb overhead. Karen did not move. Rae took her hand, and the two of them moved through the half-darkness, moved quickly and silently across the carpeted floor to the small bed. She sat on the bed and Rae sat beside her and they kissed. She turned in Rae's arms. Rae's tongue stroked Karen's lips, probing, seeking, searching. Yearning took wings and turned to passion. They clutched each other, moved on the bed, tumbling awkwardly until they were stretched out full-length upon the narrow cot, their arms around one another, their mouths drawing nourishment from each other.

While she lay there, while Rae made love to her, her hands so skillful and lips so knowing, she felt a sort of detachment that was almost schizoid in nature. A Karen Winslow was upon her back on a bed in a dark room while a beautiful blonde girl unfastened a button and worked a zipper and touched here and kissed there. That Karen Winslow felt it all and responded to it all, stirred by each kiss, provoked by each touch, drawn ever more deeply into the rhythm of passion.

But at the same time another Karen Winslow, ethereal, amorphous, sat or floated somewhere across the room, somewhere in space. And this alien Karen Winslow did not participate but merely observed, watching and knowing all while feeling nothing at all . . .

Hands touched her bare breasts, cupped them, felt their weight. Lips brushed over her lips, over her cheek, nibbled at the hollow of her throat. Moved down past her shoulder, moved down across satin skin toward the perfection of her breasts.

She had grown naked. Rae's clever hands, so quick, so gentle, had removed every stitch of Karen's clothing. The air was cool on her bare skin, cool in sharp contrast to the fire of Rae's mouth, of Rae's hands, of Rae's warm body . . .

Where their flesh touched, fire spread. Warm, glowing fire, hot coals in a campsite's residue. Ashes to ashes, lust to lust—the Karen Winslow who sat observing picked up this bit of doggerel and played with it like a cat with yarn. Ashes to ashes, lust to lust, belly to belly and breast to breast.

Somewhere the alien Karen, the untouched observer, shapeless voyeuse, went forever away. Somehow passion and desire took complete control. The well of her blood surged in her loins. Her nipples, alert with hunger, rose to Rae's lips and tingled at the touch. Her thighs trembled, sprang apart like startled fish. Her hips were caught up in a rhythm too long forgotten, a rhythm that had already been ancient when the world itself was young, rocking straining writhing rhythm of love . . .

She had wanted only to be loved. Now she yearned to love and be loved, to do and be done, to have, be had, to possess as she was in turn possessed. Her own hands sought, her own lips searched and joyfully discovered. Her hands filled themselves with Rae's breasts, twin cones of warm yielding flesh, and she thrilled alike to the feel of Rae's flesh in her hands and to the sharp intake of breath that signaled Rae's urgent excitement.

I am doing this, she thought. I am exciting this girl, this beautiful marvelous girl. I am making her happy. I am doing this, I, I . . .

The special feel of slippery flesh drawn across flesh. The sharp scent of sweat mingling magically with the odors of passion. The taste, the glorious taste, of Rae.

Their bodies moved on the bed. She was no more than barely conscious of this. Her hands, her lips, her whole body seemed to act with a will all its own. She did things without thinking of them or willing them, did things she had never known she knew how to do. It seemed as though she were proceeding by some deep instinct, as though the rituals of their lovemaking were somehow inborn. And their bodies melted and flowed together like twins streams of lava flowing down the sloping sides of a volcano.

She was a flower opening to a bee.

She was a bee draining nectar from a blossom.

Magic . . .

"I thought you would never come back, Karen."

"I couldn't stay away."

"I thought I'd scared you."

"You did. Desperately."

"The wine . . ."

"I know."

"It would have happened sooner or later. It had to. I wanted you at once, you know."

"I didn't know."

"I saw it in you when we first met. Your eyes, perhaps. I didn't trust myself. Afraid to. People see what they want to see, you know. A play I saw once—I forget the title, something in Eden—*Winter in Eden?* That sounds close enough. A musical version of Adam and Eve. In one scene Satan is tempting Eve and she says he looks like a snake, and he says *Women see snakes everywhere.* Get it? The Freudian symbol. Women see snakes because that's what they look for, only for *snakes* you read *phallic symbols.* A lovely line, really, but you have to think about it before it makes sense. Which might explain the play's monumental impact upon the world of theater. The audience walked out humming the Freudian symbols. Where was I?"

"Here. With me."

"Mmmmm. Well—people see what they look for, so I suppose I thought you were gay because I wanted you to be gay. It happens constantly downtown. You think you're getting a long-drink look from the most with-it kid since Sappho and turns out to be a devoutly heterosexual NYU coed, and the stirring stare doesn't mean she's warm for your form, just that her contact lenses are making holes in her eyes. Am I talking coherently?"

"Not especially."

"I had that feeling. Love gives me tons of things to say while it renders me utterly inarticulate. How do you feel?"

"Mmmmm."

"Happy?"

She opened her eyes, closed them again. The room was still, night outside dark and silent. Rae was curled up on the bed, her long legs tucked under her, one knee brushing but not quite touching Karen's hip. Karen lay prone on the bed with her head on a pillow. She felt somehow strange, relaxed and enervated all at once, sated and wholly content and yet on edge.

"Happy," she said at length.

"You don't sound too certain."

"But I am."

"Silly question, this, but I'll ask it. Was this your first time?"

Half a smile with eyes still shut. "The first time was a few nights ago. With you."

"Ah, yes. I knew the answer, you know. That you hadn't been with another girl before me. But I had to ask the question. I'm not an enormously secure person, dear. What was the man's name? The one who made you cut yourself?"

She opened her eyes involuntarily, moved one arm and looked at her scars. "Ronnie," she said quietly. "Why?"

"I don't know why I asked. Did you ... was it good with him? The bed part of it?"

"You want to know too much."

"I—"

"I'm sorry," she said quickly. She sighed, sat up, yawned. "That didn't come out right, mean it the way it sounded."

"I ask too damned many questions."

"It's just that I don't want to talk about it."

"I know."

"It's all . . . history, really. Do you have another cigarette?"

Rae handed her the pack. She took a cigarette out and Rae lit it for her. She drew on it, inhaled, blew out smoke, sat for a moment, then drew a second time on the cigarette. "Do you want to know something? I can't remember what it was like. I honestly cannot remember, can't picture it. Not the sex in particular. The whole affair. Living with him, the life we had, everything. I could tell you what I did and the people I knew and where I worked and how I spent days and nights, all of that. I don't mean I've lost any memories. But I can't feel it. Do you know what I mean? As though it happened long ago, ages ago, and I can't get the handle of it."

"As though it happened to somebody else?"

"Yes. Almost that way."

"It did, you know. You *were* someone else, Karen."

"Because it was before tonight?"

Rae shook her head. "No. Much as *I'd* like to take the credit for the transformation, I'm not nutty enough to believe that one little experience could work that complete a change."

"It wasn't a little experience."

"What I mean is—"

"It was a big one," she broke in.

"Clown. Braggart. No. Not because of tonight. Because of the way you were shaken up, and the way you almost killed yourself, and the way you came out of it—everything, all of it. People don't live through all of that and come out the same as they were when they started. My older brother was in the Korean War. He was eighteen when he went in and twenty when he came home, and eighteen from twenty is two, and if you think he had only aged two years in Korea then you must have rocks in your head. It was more like ten years. He looked older and he talked older and he acted older. Everything. It's not how long you live that changes you. It's what you live through."

She thought of Ted. "I have a brother," she said. "He's in the service now. Somewhere down south. I don't even know where."

"Honestly?"

She nodded. "We're not very close. I don't know why not. He's all I have left, really, but we don't keep in very close touch. He's not the type to write letters. I actually don't know where he is."

"My brother and I were very close."

"What happened?"

"He died."

"Oh, I'm sorry . . ."

"Don't be silly. It happened ten years ago. He was in one of those battles in Korea, he was shot at day after day, he killed . . . oh, too many Chinese to keep track of. I mean it was just constant slaughter from what he told me. Three times he killed men with a bayonet. He was wounded twice. All of this, you know, and nothing killed him, he got through all of it."

Rae put out her cigarette. "Then he came home and in a couple of years he died of a ruptured appendix. Isn't that ridiculous? People don't die of that any more. But his appendix ruptured without any warning and he didn't know what it was and didn't get to a hospital soon enough. They operated, and there was a postoperative infection, and they just couldn't knock it out. They always can, you know. They use antibiotics and that's the end of it. But nothing worked, and he was in that silly hospital for three weeks, and I kept telling myself that he would get better because that's what happens, people get better. Then he . . . well, then one morning he just died, actually. That's what happened. And it has never made the slightest bit of sense to me."

She looked at Rae and tried to think of something to say. The silence was overpowering but there were no words with which to break it. She had a lump in her throat and a dull pain at the back of her eyes as if she might begin to weep at any moment. She crushed out her cigarette and the moment for tears passed.

Rae said, "Well, I don't know why I got on that kick. The special Rachel Cooper finesse. Always get a love affair off on a firm footing by turning the conversation to the most morbid topic conveniently at hand. I wonder why I went on like that. I suppose it's like any old wound. You have to pick the scab from time to time to see if it still bleeds. I think it still does. Karen? Could we sort of lie together now? I just want to be held."

And then they were suddenly lying on the bed. She held Rae in her arms and felt the warmth of flesh pressing flesh. She looked into the blonde girl's eyes, and their gazes locked, and suddenly Rae began to weep. Karen held her close, very close, until she was at once crying herself. Weeping uncontrollably, shedding her tears for a nameless loss.

It was good to hold another and comfort her while she wept. It was good to be held in turn and sob out all the hurt and fear and acid that was so bad when kept too long inside. Their nakedness was sexless. Their breasts touched, their loins were in warm proximity to one another—and yet, new as this all was to her, she was entirely unconscious of any taste of passion. Sex was simply out, a part of it now just warmth and need and tenderness.

The tears came for a long time. And when they stopped there were no words. Just the closeness, the warmth.

The love.

This was love, she thought. This, she told herself, was what it really meant. Just this—far more than the kissing and stroking and the rest. Just this. This was love as she had never known it and had not even been capable of imagining it. Not what she had had with Ronnie—that seemed in retrospect like a nasty caricature of love at best. This was something new, something rather glorious.

I am in love with a girl, she thought. And incredibly enough I am not bothered by it. I do not think it is wrong or evil or awful or dirty. I am not afraid of it. I, square and unworldly Karen Winslow, am in love with a girl.

A lesbian.

No, that was too easy. She could not be so easily labeled like a bug impaled upon a pin and mounted on a board. She could not simply identify herself with a tag reading LESBIAN, a handy nametag to tell herself and the world who she was. There was more to her than that. She was not simply a lesbian. She was a girl who happened to be in love with another girl.

Her mind swam in idle circles. She was warm and comfortable and wanted to stay just as she was forever.

"I don't want to go," she murmured.

"Don't go."

"I just want to go to sleep."

"Yes."

"Like this."

"Yes."

"In your arms, like this."

"God yes."

"Rae? I love you, Rae. Isn't it fantastic? I love you, dear, darling, darling Rachel."

"I love you, too. Go to sleep, baby."

"I am in love with Rachel Cooper. Do you really hate it when I call you Rachel? I think it's a beautiful name, really. But I won't say it if you don't like it. I won't do anything you don't want me to do and I'll do absolutely nothing that you do want me to do. I am so silly. I am really very silly, you know."

"Go to sleep, silly."

"Yes. Yes, I think I will go to sleep now."

There was something else she wanted to say but she couldn't figure out just what it was. She hugged Rae tight and searched her mind for the thought and swam slowly off into sleep.

Chapter 6

The weekend was a parade with a brass band, a circus with all three rings swinging at once, a nonstop whirl that kept her head swimming. They spent every moment together, leaving the rooming house only when they had to, venturing outside to grab a quick meal around the corner or pick up cigarettes at the drug store on Saturday night, to scurry over to the liquor store on Third Avenue for a fifth of Scotch.

The bottle did not quite last through Sunday. They sat and talked and drank and made love and rested and talked and kissed and drank and made more love. It was mostly exciting and mostly wonderful. There were moments, though, when a tiny corner of Karen's private self withdrew from all of the hilarity. Now and then she would sense an element of utter insanity in all of it, a quality that would sooner or later catch up with her and drown her. Other times the clouded vision was a little less apocalyptic, and she would merely tell herself that it was not nearly so wonderful or marvelous as it seemed, that they were just two young women who found each other's company vastly preferable to loneliness and who, as an extra measure of delight, had discovered that it was oodles of delight to crawl into bed and have fun together. But neither the occasional shards of fear nor the flashes of sobriety were enough to take the edge off the thrill of it all.

She had never known her flesh could sing this way, had never dared to dream that physical love could be so enormously fine. It was not that she had ever regarded herself as frigid. She had always felt that she loved Ronnie, that she responded to him, that he fulfilled her. It only stood to reason that a frigid girl would not go live in sin with a man and fall apart at the seams when he left her. And had always rather enjoyed what they did in bed.

You don't know what love is . . .

The song ran through her head more than once that weekend. Because it was true, she had not known what love was, what it could be. She had never experienced the delight that Rae brought her, the warm security, the new passion, the deep and stirring joy.

And the love they shared was so much more even than that. She and Ronnie had rarely talked. Oh, they had spoken, had found things to say to each other, but there had never been the kind of conversation in which she felt that any real contact was being made, any genuine communication. No sense that all the wires were plugged in, no true exchange of thought and feeling.

She and Rae had this. By Sunday night, through all the drinking and laughter and love, she had told Rae everything there was to tell about herself, everything that made up the person that was Karen Winslow.

"Not very interesting," she said. "I'm afraid I haven't done much, or gone anywhere, or anything. Just plain Karen."

" . . . an ordinary guy . . ."

"Uh-huh. Not a glamorous commercial artist."

"There is very little that is glamorous in the wonderful world of commercial art."

"*You're* glamorous." She sighed. "How did you get here, Rae?"

"You have a way with the non sequitur. How did I get where?"

"Here."

"I told you last night, or were you too drunk to remember? My gym teacher corrupted me. I wanted to improve my volleyball game and she wanted to play with the two volleyballs that I kept under my sweatshirt. I was vastly overdeveloped at a tender age. Don't you recall all the gory details?"

"The scene is indelibly etched upon my memory."

"Your mammaries? It was etched on *mine*, actually."

"That's not what I meant, though. Not how-did-you-get-here figuratively, meaning how did you turn queer. I don't like the word queer. I mean how-did-you-get-here literally. Meaning here, this place, like *here*."

"New York? Everybody gets here. People wind up in New York the same way maggots wind up at the bottoms of garbage cans, and the parallel is truer the more I ponder it. I don't—"

"I mean to this precious rooming house, stupid."

"Oh. *Here*."

"That's what I said, isn't it?"

"Undeniably." Rae yawned. "Do you really want to know? We could turn off the lights and do something obscene."

"Later."

"No doubt. You really want to know?"

"Unless it's painful, my sweet." She said this last line very Bette Davis, and they broke up at once, laughing like children. It seemed to both of them like the funniest thing in the world. For weeks they would introduce the line into conversations whenever it seemed to fit, and it always made them collapse with laughter.

And, later, after laughter and after love, Rae said, "Nothing dramatic about it, kitten. Not even a shattering love affair. I've had those, God knows but not for ages. Doesn't that make me sound depressingly old? Or revoltingly depraved. You may take your pick. No, what happened was I'd been too long in the Village. It got to the point where the entire world was bordered on the north by Fourteenth Street and on the south by Houston. If I went north of Fourteenth my nose bled and if I went south of Houston I got the bends. And it was every day the same people, the same routine of gay bars and gay parties and gay clothes, everything religiously gay. We even shaved our legs with gay blades. That's a joke, sort of."

"It's terrible."

"Devastatingly awful. Well. Gay people and gay places and all, they all add up to fun for awhile. But enough is enough. For me, at least. Enough got to be too much. I found out something about myself. I found out if I let myself design my whole world around this one element of gayness I was just taking myself and putting myself in a box marked *queer*. I was making that the whole body and soul of life, see? I was a lesbian first and Rae Cooper second, and I was having none of it. It's a very convenient copout, being gay is, said the nice lady."

"You lost me."

"Don't you see? Not that there's a particular reason why you should. But look—you can take that one label, *Gay*, and you can put it on yourself and excuse every other part of your life. You concentrate everything upon all the special areas of homosexuality. You pity yourself for being a member of a depressed minority group. It really knocks me out the way all of the faggots keep screaming for equal rights. That's the battle cry—freedom now. It would kill most of them, Karen. And it would kill us, too. We wouldn't be able to pity ourselves. Or laugh at all the 'in' jokes that are only funny because no one else gets them. Or . . . oh, I don't know. Is any of this making any sense?"

She nodded.

"I was in an apartment, on Waverly Place. Between engagements, you might say. My lease came up for renewal, and I decided that I just did not want to stay there any more. The place was too big for me, and I'd blown all the money I'd saved up because I was going through this awful lazy period and not taking any work and just spending what I'd saved, and I couldn't afford to pay rent on the place by myself any more. And I wasn't about to fall in love at the drop of a skirt just to get half my rent paid. You'd be surprised how often that happens. There's nothing like an unbreakable lease on an expensive mausoleum to make a girl ready for love. It's amazing. I think apartment leases are the most powerful aphrodisiacs of modern gay society.

"Well. I got out of there and couldn't find anything I wanted, and then it came to me that I wasn't going to find what I wanted in the Village or Brooklyn Heights or any of the usual places, because I had a yen to get clear of all the old haunts. I'd been staying in hotels while I was figuring all of this out, and then I decided it was about time to get something a little more permanent than a hotel, and I wound up here. See what happens when you ask a very simple question, baby? You get a sermon for an answer."

"I love you, Rae."

"That's a nice baby."

"I do."

"It won't be forever, Karen."

"Don't say that."

"It won't though. Nothing ever is. *Nothing is forever, always is a lie.* You remember the song?"

"Yes, I do,"

"Pure poetry, and pure truth."

"Do you remember the next line? In the song?"

"Not offhand."

"*I can only love you till the day I die,*" Karen said. "That's close to forever, isn't it?"

"Ah." A soft, lazy smile. "Perhaps."

Rae was still sleeping in the morning when she left for her job. Leon Gordon's new office, she discovered, was significantly more impressive than his old one. New steel furniture replaced the battered oak desk and chair she remembered in the office where she first met the theatrical agent, and the office was located in a better building at a more impressive address. But Gordon himself looked and sounded the same.

"You're here," he said. 'That's good. That desk'll be here, you'll sit right there, see? There's two rooms, this one here which is the anteroom and my own office in back. I've been trying to figure out what's the best way to use you. What I want you for is something classy to sit behind the desk and to pick up the phone when it rings. But there's other things. I've got this place fixed up pretty cute. Here, sit down there, got it?"

She sat down behind the desk.

"Now there's two things you got to do. One is when the phone rings, and you pick it up and say, 'LeGo Associates, good morning.' Or good afternoon or whatever the hell it is. Then when they ask for me you ask who's calling, and you say just a minute, please, and you press the button which is Hold. See?"

"I see."

"Then there's this switch on the side of the desk. Underneath. Find it?"

He pointed out the switch for her. "You flick this," he said, "and there's a quick buzz in my office and the lines open up and I can hear whatever you say out here. Then when you tell me who it is on the phone, and I say whether I'm in or not. If I'm in, I take the call, or otherwise you get rid of him. You got that?"

"Yes."

"It's a funny thing," he said. "A friend of mine, he books a lot of very big jazz musicians, also some of the newer folksingers. He hired this one girl and I thought he was going to go off his nut. The trouble was she couldn't tell a lie. A little George Washington. It would bother her to say he was out when he was in, and either she just told people the truth or she would blurt around like a nut and they would wonder what the hell was up. It made her uncomfortable, lying. A very religious girl, and Sam hated to fire her, but what do you do? You get me? She was doing him no good at all, but at the same time she was willing to work, she was a nice kid, and how the hell could he come out and fire her because she was honest? See?"

She nodded.

"You don't mind that kind of lying, do you?" She assured him that she didn't. "Because it's necessary in this business. All right, that's how it goes with the phone calls. Now when somebody—"

The phone rang. He started to reach for it, then stopped himself. "You might as well learn right away," he said. "Answer it."

She picked up the phone. "LeGo Associates," she said, her voice crisply efficient and professional. "Good morning." A female voice wanted to speak with Leon. "Who's calling, please?" The caller identified herself. "One moment, please," she said.

She pressed the *Hold* button and turned to Gordon. "It's—"

"The switch," he said. "The intercom switch."

"But you're right here," she said.

"Just so you get the hang of it."

She threw the switch. "Miss Marla Harriman, Mister Gordon," she said.

"I'll talk to her," he said.

And, after he had told Marla Harrison that he had not heard from someone named Prager, but that he would be in touch with her as soon as anything popped, he told Karen she had done very well. "A good telephone manner," he said. "Very important. Now with people walking right into the office you do about the same, only different. As soon as they come in you flip the switch, and that way I can hear the whole conversation. If it's somebody which you don't know, and they'll all be like that at the start, you make sure they say their names loud and clear. Or otherwise you greet them and mention their name, so either way I know who it is. Sometimes it can be a lot of trouble to duck people you would rather not talk to, and who needs the aggravation, and if you come into the office to ask me and then come out and tell them I'm out they know I'm just ducking them, and it's a headache, believe me. Now, do you see those two bulbs on the desk?"

She looked. There were two bulbs on the desk top, one red and one green.

"When I hear the name, I'll flash you. A red means get rid of the bum, a green means send him right on in. That way anybody who gets sent away is sure it's on the up-and-up. I had to get all of this specially designed. I paid for it, believe me, but you couldn't ask for a better system. You think you understand how it works?"

"I think so."

"You seem like a pretty sharp girl, I'll admit that. And a very good voice on the telephone. You handle the calls and the creeps that walk into the office and you do that properly and I'll tell you the truth, there's not an awful lot of other work to do. There's a typewriter on your desk but you probably won't use it more than once a week if that. I'm funny, I got in the habit of typing all my own letters. So if you just answer the phone and the rest of it, that's enough. You get the picture?"

"Yes," she said.

"Good." He grabbed his hat, a dark gray fedora with the crown slightly crushed in front. "I've got to see a guy," he said. "I'll be back in forty minutes or an hour. Anybody calls, you tell 'em I'm out."

"I'll do that," she said.

～⋅∘⋅∘～

She had not thought the job would be terribly taxing but it was even easier than she had guessed. Gordon was gone most of the morning. There were about a dozen calls, and she told each caller that the agent was out and tried to get a message. When there were messages she typed them up on 3x5 index cards and placed them on his desk.

Three times the office door opened that morning. A messenger left a package, a very tall and very thin blonde asked for Gordon and left without giving her name when she learned he was out, and a stately middle-aged man paused in the doorway, smiled brightly at her, and told her that she improved the agent's office immeasurably.

He looked astonishingly familiar but she could not place him at first. He was tall and slender, with black hair combed straight back, gray at the temples. His nose was long and hawk-like, his eyes brightly blue. He said something she didn't hear, and then she blurted out, "Oh, you're Judge Randall!"

"Fantastic," the man said.

She blushed profoundly. "I'm sorry," she said. "I knew you looked familiar, and then I remembered—"

"Judge Philip Randall," he intoned. "Linda's understanding uncle on *As Time Goes By*. To be known for that . . . But it does sell a lot of soap, doesn't it? Shakespeare never sold soap, the poor soul, so that's a point in our favor. Edwin Booth never sold soap, Jack Barrymore never sold soap."

She was still blushing. He smiled disarmingly. "Don't redden so. I'm actually quite delighted to be Judge Randall, and equally delighted to be recognized at all. Your employer is a diamond in the truly rough but his heart is pure. And his skill is enormous, getting steady work for an old has-been. An old has-been by the unlikely name of Adrian March, to be specific. Is Leon in?"

"No, I'm afraid he's out, Mister March."

"A pity. Tell him—let me think, now—tell him I came by, and it was nothing urgent, but that Slade wants me for a commercial and he should get in touch with him. And that I got the impression they want me rather badly, though I fail to see how I can persuade a clutch of frustrated housewives to use Flem in their automatic washers. Or whatever idiocy they're selling. Can you remember that?"

"Yes, Mister March."

"And tell him also that he's engaged a perfectly charming girl, albeit one who's a bit out of place in the employ of so ill-bred a lad as Leon. Be sure you tell him that. It's ever so much more important than a television commercial. I didn't see you here at all last week, and I was here Friday. Did you just start work?"

"This morning."

"And your name is . . ."

"Karen," she said. "Karen Winslow."

"Poetry," Adrian March said. "Echoes of Winslow Homer paintings mingled with a shiver of lush Scandinavian blondeness. Your name, that is. Karen Winslow." He sighed theatrically. "Oh, to be young again. Or even to be forty again. Or fifty, or sixty."

"You're not sixty—"

"Don't step on my lines, Karen Winslow. Do you have the message?" She parroted it back to him. "Extraordinary," he said. "Beauty combined with flawless efficiency. Remarkable in one so young."

She was blushing and grinning at once. It was time for a fast curtain, and the actor knew as much. He swept out the door and closed it after him. She sat for a moment, thinking how remarkable it was to actually meet Judge Randall. Adrian March, she corrected herself. Adrian March.

She typed his message on a neat white card and placed it on Gordon's desk.

～ ◦•◦ ～

The first week was an odd combination of nervous hurrying and long periods of nothing at all to do. Gordon managed to stay out of the office two or three hours a day and spent the rest of his time on the telephone. Sometimes the phone would ring constantly and she would have to field one call after the next, making sure that the right ones got through and the wrong ones did not. Other times the phone would remain placidly silent. Some hours there was an endless parade of clients to the office of LeGo Associates, and she would play the usual merry games with Gordon's intercom system. Now and then something would go horribly wrong—once Gordon hit the wrong button by accident and had to go chasing down the hall to catch an important young singer before she disappeared into the elevator, and once she forgot to press the Hold button and a newspaper columnist got the special treat of hearing Gordon bellow out: "Listen, make a note of this—I'm always out when that son of a bitch calls."

But generally things went well, and she found that the job suited her perfectly. She had thought that the pressure might be difficult; instead she was delighted to learn that she thrived on it. And when no one came into the office, and when the telephone was oddly silent, and when Gordon himself was out and not apt to burst in on her to ask how to spell a word or whether it was *who* or *whom* that he should be using—during those quiet times she could sit at her desk with a book or newspaper and relax entirely.

The job was fine and fulfilling.

The evenings, away from the office, were infinitely richer. Because her life was rapidly becoming bound up in Rae, and the love that had blossomed between them was ripening steadily. Day after day she waited for something to go wrong, waited for her mind to reel at the thought that what she and Rae did was wrong, that it was evil, perverse. But this was something that she could not believe at all, and so the thought refused to come to trouble her.

Instead she grew progressively more convinced of the utter rightness of the love they had. She was not about to run through the streets enlisting converts to lesbianism. Nor was she about to dress in slacks and mannish jackets to announce her predilection to the world. It was something private, and there was no reason why it should not remain that way. Before, when she lived with Ronnie, she had not worn a button proclaiming I AM A HETEROSEXUAL, and an inverse proclamation would be at least as ridiculous.

But what she felt was not shame. Never that.

Love.

It was love, genuine love, and that was simply all there was to it. No—she corrected herself—it was more than love, ever so much more than love. It was, in addition, feeling at long last of belonging entirely to the world in which she lived, the special private and personal world she inhabited. And it was this feeling that made her realize, perhaps for the first time, just how very much she had come so very close to losing when she sliced the razor blade across each of her wrists in turn.

Life seemed little enough to lose at the time. And death, however fearful and unknowable, is less terrible when life has nothing to offer. But now, now, she lived in love and loved life, and she would wake up shaking at the thought of having almost succeeded in the awful business of suicide.

The job was part of her satisfaction, part of the world she belonged in. But she did not kid herself. She knew that Rae and Rae's love were the major factors.

Not just . . . not just the bed part, she thought. There were times when it was sheer heaven, times when it was so good she could not believe it was really happening. But by the end of the week, after the initial thrill of fresh discovery had somewhat abated, the sex part was not so constant a part of their relationship. They slept together every night—always in Rae's room—and they made love every night, but by Friday they had stopped flying at one another whenever the opportunity presented itself. They actually left the building now and then—to a movie Thursday night, for a walk earlier in the week. The sexual side of their life was better than ever, and every night they found out new things about each other, found more delightful ways of making love. But now the rest of their love was ripening, too, and she liked it even better that way.

Friday afternoon she sat at the desk in the LeGo Associates office and studied the real estate advertisements in that morning's copy of the *Times*. For several days now she had wanted to look at the listings of apartments for rent, and each time she had forced herself to skip the listings because she knew what it would mean. Some of the things that Rae had said stuck in her mind. She remembered phrases about girls who fell in love with one another so that they could split the rent. She remembered that Rae had moved to the rooming house to get away from that whole rat race.

But suppose they took an apartment in an ordinary neighborhood, not in one of the standard refuges for lesbians and male homosexuals. Suppose they found an apartment right in the neighborhood where they were already living, a small but comfortable place in the general vicinity of Gramercy Park. Nothing expensive, nothing very fancy. Just something generally pleasant.

A bedroom, a living room, and a kitchen. That was all they

needed. And one big bed, but not so big that they would have trouble finding each other . . .

They could share an apartment for not much more than they were paying to rent their two unlovely rooms in the Nineteenth Street rooming home. And cooking their own food would mean a good saving, too. And it would certainly be easier for Rae to work if she had a larger, more comfortable place to work in. In one room she had now, she had to get out every hour or so or the walls seemed to be closing in on her. How could she get any decent work done in a place like that?

In an apartment, their own apartment, there would be no furtive creeping, no sneaking from one room to the other, no need to be careful about noise so that someone on the other side of the paper-thin wall would not know that they were in bed together, making wild and wonderful love together, mouth to mouth and flesh on flesh. She would not have to sneak out of Rae's room at dawn like a guilty adulterer. She could come and go with her head held high.

Still she knew how Rae felt, knew what Rae would say. *Nothing is forever. Always is a lie. And leases run for a minimum of a year, and in a year you might not even remember what I look like, kitten. It goes that way sometimes . . .*

∿•∿

They had dinner at the Italian restaurant. She drank more wine than usual but she was learning lately how to drink without letting it loosen her tongue. They almost always had wine with their meals, and Rae generally kept a bottle of Scotch in her room, and she was learning to get a little alcoholic edge on without letting the alcohol get control of her. So she didn't even mention her idea to Rae. She kept thinking about it, but she didn't let out a word.

And over coffee Rae said, "This is crazy damn foolishness. Karen, but I was thinking."

"What's so crazy about thinking?"

"About us."

"Oh?"

"Mmmm. Shall I tell you?"

"Unless it's painful, my sweet," she said, with their usual Bette Davis inflection. They laughed, loud and happy, and people turned to stare at them but they did not care at all.

"It was a silly thought," Rae said.

"Tell me."

"Oh, you know. I just, well, I was sitting in that damned room and thinking what a prison a room like that can turn into, and how much cheaper it would be in the long run if we shared a place, and . . ."

Saturday they picked up the early bird edition of the Sunday *Times*. They scanned it together and spent the afternoon hunting. By Sunday afternoon they had signed the lease. It took four nights to furnish the new apartment. Friday they moved in.

Chapter 7

They sat together on the new deep purple couch. There was classical music on the radio, something by Dvorak. The only thing she knew by Dvorak was the "New World Symphony", and this wasn't it, so she wasn't sure what they were listening to. And did not very much care.

"I'm not sure about that print."

"You don't like it there?" she said.

"I'm not sure. Maybe the other wall."

"Over the chair? We tried it there already and you hated it. Don't you remember?"

"I remember."

"Then . . ."

"Oh, forget it, Karen."

"My point exactly."

"I can't believe we managed everything that quickly, that's all. Usually it takes hellishly long to find a place. And then when you find something one of you likes it and the other one doesn't, and you fight, and then you finally take something that neither of you is too crazy about, and you both drag all your junk in and nothing matches."

"It's a good thing we're compatible."

"Because this way we've managed to produce a decorator's dream, haven't we?"

"Oh, we surely have."

Actually, they hadn't; few decorator's dreams emerge from the Salvation Army furniture store. But the apartment looked surprisingly good in spite of the little they had spent on furniture. The bed was decent, of course, and they had bought a fairly good couch. Everything else was secondhand, and looked it, but the room went together nicely nevertheless, achieving an effect that was more comfortable than shabby, more lived-in than lived-to-death.

The apartment was not far from the rooming house. They had a second-floor walkup in a brownstone on 22nd Street just a few doors east of Third Avenue. The neighborhood was a good one still and the building itself was decently maintained. Their place was tiny—a small bedroom, a small living room, a bathroom with a tub you had to pleat yourself in order to fit in, a kitchen that was a joke. But it would do. It was large enough so that Rae could set up a small drawing table in the corner of the living room near the front window, large enough so that they could spend time in it without going stir crazy. And most important of all, it was theirs and theirs alone.

"I think we'll like it here, Karen."

"I know we will," she said. She picked the bottle up from the coffee table and poured a little Scotch into her glass. She was getting a wee bit tight, she thought. Just a little bit high and happy.

"Ready for a refill?"

"I've still got a full glass. Don't go getting smashed on me, will you?"

"Don't worry." She lifted her glass, drank off about a third of her drink. "It's just that I'm happy, and I want to feel as happy as I can. But I won't get *too* drunk."

"I hope not."

"In fact—" she drained her glass "—I think I'm beginning to feel just about perfect."

"No more creeping down the halls," Rae said.

"Or being careful not to jangle the bedsprings."

"Actually, they didn't exactly jangle. It was more of a creak."

"Sort of a cree-yickkkk, cree-yickkk."

"Uh-huh."

Rae settled close to her, and Karen put an arm around the blonde girl. Rae's face settled against the side of Karen's full breast. She was wearing a nubby yellow sweater and a black skirt. Rae wore lime stretch pants and a black tailored blouse. Karen put a hand on Rae's leg and stroked the taut green material and felt the gentle swell of the flesh beneath it.

"You know what?"

"What?"

"I'd like to open your pants."

"Don't talk dirty, kitten."

"I feel a little dirty. I feel very coarse and vulgar. You know what I want to do?"

"Karen . . ."

"I'll whisper it in your ear." She put her lips to the blonde girl's ear, blew into her ear, kissed it, then whispered something softly.

"Oh . . ."

"Uh-huh."

She kissed Rae, drew the girl close, held her tight in her arms so that their breasts were pressed together and their arms were around each other. She was the leader now and the older and more experienced girl was the follower. She was the initiator, the aggressor, and she quivered with excitement at the feel of Rae's firm female body and the taste of her eager mouth.

They made love slowly, languorously. Like kids in the back seat of a car, she thought. Like a couple of teenagers parking by the lake to watch the midnight submarine races.

Her hand moved, cupped the fullness of Rae's breast through the fabric of the blouse and the bra beneath it. She flexed the firm flesh, rubbed, patted, petted, stroked, and was rewarded with little sighs and gasps from Rae. Her hand dropped to Rae's leg and she stroked the long limb slowly and rhythmically from knee to top of thigh stopping just short of the home of love, coming closer each time, closer, closer . . .

Her own head swam slightly with the liquor she had had. It didn't bother her. She closed her eyes and felt a delicious flush of dizziness overwhelm her, then subside lingeringly. She kissed Rae, and Rae's lips parted to admit Karen's probing tongue. She drank the sweetness of the girl's lovely mouth, drank deep, and her fingers moved to toy with the buttons on the front of the tailored blouse.

It was, she knew, a complete reversal of the way it had been the first time with them. Now she was entirely active, Rae wholly passive. They had no butch-and-femme relationship, nothing so clearly defined. Instead their lovemaking each time assumed the pattern that fit the occasion, the rhythm that suited their mood. The mood now was ideal. Rae leaned back in her arms, stretched out full length upon the couch. Karen crouched over her, unfastened the last button, drew the blouse out from the waistband of the stretch pants.

She drew a sharp breath, then dipped her head low to let her tongue race over the silken flesh of Rae's stomach.

Rae purred. Karen got her hands behind the older girl's back, fumbled the bra open. She drew the straps down over Rae's shoulders and cast the bra aside.

With her clever fingers, she teased Rae's breasts into turgid awareness, stopping only to nuzzle the two globes of flesh with lips and tongue. And she talked constantly, her voice an urgent whisper as she spoke every filthy word she knew, mouthing obscenities she had never used in her life.

She paused once to pour more Scotch into her glass and drink it off. Then she took off Rae's stretch pants, easing them down over the rounded hips. Down, all the way down and off. The blonde girl wore nothing beneath them.

In the darkness of her mind's eye she saw, suddenly and in awesome clarity, an image that tore and twisted at her. A girl naked in a naked room, a frightened girl, with a razor blade in her hand, a girl using a razor blade to make experimental red lines upon her pale wrist. Someone screamed inside her head, and all at once it was gone, all of it . . .

Her hands moved furiously over Rae's warm body, touching, probing, finding. Karen did not even take the time to remove her own clothes. She felt driven, oddly and inexplicably possessed. As if she had to bear witness, as if she had to prove herself, as if, somehow, she had to overcome.

Her hair brushed over Rae's breasts. The blonde girl, still wholly passive, moaned and sighed beneath her skilled caresses. Karen sucked at her breasts like a greedy infant, rubbed her face over the silken bounty of Rae's stomach.

Down . . .

There was no moon, there were no stars, there was only the yin and the yang, the alpha and the omega of a burning, brutal, bitter kiss.

ᘒ•ᘖ

"Rae? I'm sorry, Rae."

"Sorry? For what?"

"Whatever I did."

"Don't be silly."

"I thought it was good for us. I thought it . . . I thought it was good, but it wasn't, was it?"

"It was fine, darling."

"I don't think so."

"Why?"

"I . . . I don't know."

"I had a good time, Karen, if that's what you mean."

"No, I—"

"It was just that things seemed a little vicious there for a little while. As though you had to show me something. As though there was something pretty loveless about what we were doing, and it's nothing, honey, and I know it's nothing, but it put me in a mood for no good reason at all and I got a little sulky. I'm sorry, Karen."

She said nothing. She wanted to freshen her drink but the bottle was too far for her to reach it and she didn't have the strength to get up and get it.

"Karen?"

She didn't answer.

"Poor baby. I was afraid you were drinking too much. You're

out on your feet and you don't know it. We'd better go to bed, love. Come with me."

In a fog, she let Rae help her to her feet and guide her from the living room to the bedroom. Rae had to help her undress. It was an eerie feeling. She felt entirely sober, fully awake, but she had trouble getting her sweater off and couldn't negotiate the clasp on her skirt, and Rae had to help her. And she thought she was perfectly aware of what was going on, but then she would lose track of things from one minute to the next. Rae was right, she told herself; she was a lot drunker than she seemed to realize.

"My poor girl," she heard Rae say. "Easy, now. I'd tell you that you'll feel better in the morning except that I have the feeling that you won't, not at all. You'll probably have one hell of a head on you. If you wake up and feel rotten, you wake me right away, do you hear me, baby? You wake me and I'll see what I can do to help you. Do you understand?"

"Yes."

"Will you remember? I have a feeling you won't remember anything I'm saying to you, Karen."

"Huh?"

Soft laughter. "Easy, baby." Lips that brushed her own, strong hands that eased her down onto her pillow. "Sleep. Sleep like a drunken lamb, baby . . ."

~•~

She woke early. Rae was still sleeping and she let her sleep, moving noiselessly from bedroom to bathroom and gulping a few aspirins. Her head ached; other than that she was fine. Before long the aspirins had taken care of the headache and she was in perfect shape, not nearly as wretched as she had expected she would be. It surprised and delighted her. When you could drink that much and get that looped and still wake up without a hangover, she thought, it made perfectly good sense to become an alcoholic.

She scribbled a brief note for Rae. *Feeling fine, didn't want to wake you, thought I'd go for a walk, back soon. Love, Karen.* She read the note over, thinking that it was fairly absurd to sign it. Even without a signature Rae would probably have little trouble figuring out who had written it. She read it to herself a second time without punctuation and decided that the closing was not a signature but a plea—not "Love, Karen," but "Love Karen"—an order.

Do, she thought. Do love me.

She left the note on the bathroom mirror, dressed, ran a comb through her hair, scooped up her purse and hurried downstairs and outside. The air was cool and scented fresh, although she knew that there was really no such thing as fresh air in New York. She walked to the corner, bought a newspaper, walked halfway down the block on Third Avenue and found an open lunch counter. She went inside, took a stool at the counter and ordered a plate of ham and eggs, a short glass of orange juice, an order of toast and a cup of black coffee.

Her appetite surprised her, and she wolfed her food and settled down with a cigarette and a second cup of coffee. It seemed almost unholy to feel so very fine after such an excessive evening. Too much drinking, too much of the wrong sort of love, too much of everything, and yet she felt better than she had ever felt in her life.

There almost had to be a moral there.

Live it up, she decided. Maybe that was the magic answer—live it up, live life to the hilt, do what you want to do when you want to do it, and to hell with worry and fear and fright and nerves and all the little curses that drove little people to little graves in gigantic cemeteries. *Live it up.* Drink when thirsty, eat when hungry, love then lustful, sleep when tired, and die when ready.

A credo.

And not a bad one at that, she told herself. Not so very bad at all. Guilt and fear and worry put razor cuts on pale wrists in lonely rooms. She had been that route, and she knew, and she would not walk that road again.

Her job was a good one. She enjoyed it and handled it well, and each day she met more of Gordon's clients and felt more at ease with them and with him. The girls, mostly tall blonde busty types, were mostly friendly. The men—there were fewer of them—made casual passes now and then, more as a matter of form than out of any desperate craving for her fair white body. And the passes did not unsettle her, not any more.

So the job was fine. And the home life was also fine, if she merely relaxed and let it be at its best, let herself enjoy what was there to be enjoyed.

Eat, drink, be merry . . .

For tomorrow we live, she thought. So eat and drink and be merry so that there will be something worth living for.

Chapter 8

"You look radiant," Rae said.

"I should."

"Oh?"

"I had lunch out today." She drew on her cigarette, set it down in an ashtray, blew out smoke. "That bolsters one's morale," she added.

They were in the Dappled Door, a Third Avenue restaurant that served passable open sandwiches and very good cocktails. Rae was drinking a Scotch sour, Karen a Rob Roy.

"You always have lunch out," Rae said. "You can't make do with a sandwich at your desk. That wouldn't go with that note of class that your employer strives to protect."

"I had lunch with a man."

"Oh?"

"Uh-huh. Jealous?"

"Who was it? Your judge friend?"

"Uh-huh. Jealous?"

"I guess I'm supposed to be, aren't I?" The blonde girl crushed out a cigarette. "I'm afraid I can't get awfully worked up about it, kitten. In the first place, you've had lunch with him before. In the second place, he's old enough to be your—"

"Older lover," Karen supplied helpfully.

"Father, is what I was going to say. Trite but true. And in the third place—"

"Are there many more places left?"

"This is the last one. In the third place, I don't think he's exactly your type."

"Who is?"

"I am," Rae said.

"We dined in style. L'Aiglon, no less."

"Very fancy."

"Uh-huh. I really like his company, Rae. You know it's—" she fumbled for the words "—it's nice having a man that you can like and can talk to and that you can be completely comfortable with, do you know what I mean?"

"I know."

"Without any sex thing coming into the picture. I mean, we're good friends and we can certainly talk about things and all . . ."

"Thanks a bunch."

"Oh, you know what I mean, don't you? It's good to be friends with a man, but it would be bad if there were any sex thing. And most of the time there is, I guess. They always make passes unless they're too old or something. Even if they aren't really interested, they always throw you a pass, and it can spoil things."

"All but the lesbian's dream trio."

"Who are they? The lame and the halt and the blind?"

"That's not bad," Rae said. "I was thinking of the relatives, the old ones, and the faggots."

"I'll drink to that," Karen said.

"You'll drink to almost anything."

There was the echo of an edge to Rae's voice. Karen carefully ignored it. "I haven't been drinking any more," she said.

"You haven't been drinking any less, either."

"I think we've got the beginning of a pretty fair vaudeville routine. Vas you effer in Zinzinnati?"

"Positively, Mister Shean."

There were times, as the weeks passed, when she wondered what Adrian March saw in her. They drifted gradually into the habit of getting together once or twice a week for lunch, always in a good restaurant, always with March picking up the check. At first she had tried to pay her own way but he wouldn't let her.

"There are only two good aspects to playing the rancid role of Judge Philip Randall and peddling detergents to the Great Unwashed," he had told her. "One is that the work is steady and easy, and the other is that one makes a surprising amount of money. Even good living fails to dispose of the money faster than it accrues. If I let you pay your own way, Karen, one of several possible things would happen. You might find excuses to avoid lunching with me due to an inability to afford expensive lunches. Or I might stop asking you out of an unwillingness to impose a financial burden upon you. Or, worst of all, we might take to dining in foul little budget-minded restaurants and foregoing the pleasure of a cocktail before dinner. I am far too hedonistic to make that sacrifice for the sake of your misplaced pride. Humor an antique actor, my dear. Let me pick up all the tabs."

After that she had not mentioned the subject again. She didn't have to—they never seemed to run out of things to talk about. He knew almost everyone in the theater, or at least it seemed that way to her, and he was an endless source of anecdotes and inside information. More than that, he talked about anything and everything with her, from politics and such to fairly abstract philosophical arguments.

This was something she had missed for far too long. She had always been a bright girl, at least a borderline intellectual. All during college she had lived for the real, meaningful conversation that was as important a part of college as the lectures and reading and examinations. But when she lived with Ronnie all of that somehow withered away. Ronnie did not converse with a person, he *played* to the person, making every talk an audition. And, she thought now, he had always been a bad actor.

Even with Rae, there was no real opportunity for conversation. She felt disloyal when the realization first came to her, but it was true nevertheless. With Rae, their talk was always profoundly personal. Despite all their rapport, they could not seem to talk at length about anything outside of their own small if comfortable world. Broader topics were invariably reduced to trivia or else merely flirted with.

At times this bothered her but most of the time she was able to shrug it off with little difficulty. She and Rae had a good, fine, firm relationship. They loved each other, they were happy with each other. No relationship could be utterly perfect in every way. Theirs came close enough to satisfy her.

If only Rae didn't keep harping on one subject.

Her drinking.

There was no getting around it, she had to admit. She *was* drinking more, and was having drinks more frequently. When she lunched with Adrian March, they always had a drink before the meal, often two and occasionally three. Even with a heavy lunch on top of the cocktails, she would get high enough to feel the effect of the liquor through the afternoon. It didn't seem to affect her work adversely. If anything, it relaxed her and made her feel more at ease on the job. If she had three drinks, though, she did have a tendency to make typographical errors more readily than usual. But that was about the only place where it showed. Other than that, she could function at least as well with an edge on as she could when she was stone cold sober.

She was less and less often stone cold sober. She and Rae always had drinks after work, at the apartment. It was a ritual, and certainly a good one—a line of demarcation between the work day and the evening, especially valuable for Rae, who worked at the apartment and could stand a sharp break between work and relaxation.

If they went out for dinner, which they did a few nights a week, they generally had wine with their meals. They often drank wine at home when Rae cooked. The blonde girl did not like to cook often, but when she did put on apron she generally made a production out of it, and there was something moderately nauseating in the idea of sitting down to a sumptuous spread of, say, Beef Bourguignon, without a bottle of good Pommard on the table.

Bit by bit, she kept finding new ways in which alcohol proved itself valuable and then became indispensable. She discovered, for example, that it was a very fine thing to sip a little cognac while reading a book or listening to the FM radio; before long, it was almost impossible to pick a decent book or dial in some music without spilling a taste of cognac into a small snifter and paying at least as much attention to the cognac as to the book or music. And the cocktail-before-lunch routine with Adrian March led her to the happy discovery that one could have a cocktail before lunch even when one dined alone. After all, a meal in a decent restaurant was unthinkable without a martini or sour to sharpen the palate. Some of the time she ate at a hamburger place where no liquor was served, but more and more often she found herself going to the Brass Rail and sharpening her palate with something around eighty or ninety proof.

Harvey's Bristol Cream, she found, was nice after a meal. Better than dessert, and less fattening.

Coffee with Irish Whiskey in it, she learned, tasted much better than coffee with cream and sugar in it. And didn't seem like drinking at all, since, after all, it was only coffee, wasn't it?

"It's not as though I had a problem," she told Adrian March one lunch hour. "It would be different if I got drunk, but I don't. Have you ever seen me stoned?"

"No, but I see you fairly early in the day, Karen. Do you get drunk at night?"

"Only if I have a lot to drink."

"That's an extraordinary observation. Do you ever have blackouts? Ever wake up with a fuzzy memory? Or are you crystal clear the day after a binge?"

"I don't really have binges, for one thing." She gnawed the tip of one finger. "And I don't get hangovers. Sometimes I'll wake up with a headache, but never anything that a couple of aspirin won't fix in a minute or two. Sometimes I won't remember the details, say, of the last half hour before I went to sleep. Why? Does that mean something?"

"It can. It's supposed to be a sign that alcohol hits you harder than you think. But just losing a half hour isn't that remarkable, especially when you're half-unconscious during that half-hour to begin with."

"It's not as if I *have* to drink . . ."

"My dear," March said archly, "everyone has to drink. The alternative is utter sobriety and that would be unthinkable."

"I could stop if I wanted to. But why stop something that I enjoy?"

"Exactly."

"I'm certainly not an *alcoholic.*"

"What's an alcoholic?"

"How do I define it?" She thought a moment. "Someone who can't handle liquor at all. That's the way I understand it. Someone who takes one drink and keeps on drinking until he passes out, with no control. He can go for months without touching a drop, but one shot puts him off on a binge right away. Is that the way it goes or have I been watching too many movies?"

March smiled. "I suppose that's a valid definition," he said. "But I'm not like that at all, you know. I can drink without going on binges."

"Well, you're certainly not an alcoholic, Adrian."

"Oh, but I certainly am."

She stared at him.

"I drink," he said, "slowly but steadily from morning until night, spacing a precarious line of shot glasses from cradle to grave. Do you know the line from *Prufrock?* 'I have measured out my life with coffee spoons.' A marvelous phrase. I have measured out my life with shot glasses, and cocktail glasses, and wine glasses . . ."

"I've never seen you drunk, Adrian."

"You've never seen me sober, either. Didn't you realize as much?" He shook his head in wonder. "I haven't had a sizable blackout in ten or fifteen years, which is why I don't place too much credence in that definition of alcoholism. I have hangovers, but I've learned to get ready for them—aspirin the night before, thiamine during the day, aspirin and fruit juice on awakening, a little milk of magnesia after breakfast. You ought to be writing this down."

"Why?"

"You may find the information useful, Karen. Don't look so horrified. Do you have any idea how many people drink too much? And can't get along without it? And function in spite of it?" He set down his cigarette, then picked it up and drew on it again. "I have not had a wholly sober breath since my wife died fourteen years ago. Fifteen years, come to think of it. That's not what set me off, I was drinking regularly enough before then, but when she died it only seemed reasonable and proper to sober up for the funeral. So I stayed dry for a few days, which was not so hard as I thought it might be but not much fun either, and then I started again." He spread his hands. "There you have it. My public would be horrified but—" he smiled knowingly "Judge Philip Randall is a lush."

"I never would have guessed," she said.

"Perhaps I hide it well. An actor has that power Burns wrote of, seeing himself as others see him. In the theater the impression is of paramount importance, the reality a bad second. Any producer on Broadway would rather employ an actor who drinks but doesn't show it than one who makes do with two rum cokes a month but muffs his lines whenever he smells the cork."

"Could you stop?"

"Perhaps. May I beg the question? If I wanted to badly enough,

I could stop. People can do anything if they want to badly enough. I obviously don't want to, not with any basic desire. And on top of that—oh, look at the time."

"Oh, I'm late."

"You go ahead," he said. "I'll take care of the tab."

That afternoon she sat at her desk and thought that no one person should have to support more than a single vice. It wasn't decent, and you couldn't carry it off in style. It was enough to be a lesbian. She couldn't hack piling alcoholism on top of homosexuality. You had to take your choice, had to decide whether you wanted to be a lesbian or a lush; you couldn't be both at once.

It was ridiculous, she told herself. She was no alcoholic.

She was simply a person who liked a drink at certain times of the day, or on certain occasions.

Still . . .

She had never done much drinking before. What was responsible? Not her state of mind, certainly, because she was happier and more gratified than she had ever been before. Not her body chemistry, either, since it was fairly obvious that she was not the one-drink-and-away-we-go type of lush. No matter how she looked at it, it seemed a clear-cut thing—she drank when she wanted to because she liked the taste of it and the effect it had upon her. She drank more now than in the past because in the past she had not known what a pleasant difference a drink could make, nor would her former self have had the courage to indulge herself whenever and however she wanted to.

But it was not as though she needed it.

Why not prove it to herself? She would simply not have a drink for the next three days. Nothing—no wine, no beer, no cocktails, no Scotch, nothing at all. She would not make any announcements of the fact, no grand vows. She would just quit for a few days to prove she could do it with no stress and no strain at all; then once it had been proved to her satisfaction, she could live her life the way she chose.

The first night wasn't too hard. They ate at home, just sandwiches that Rae had thrown together. Rae was working on a batch of preliminary sketches and was too wrapped up in what she was doing to care about doing to care about going out for dinner or to prepare anything elaborate. She managed to avoid the standard before-dinner drink as well; she took the drink but poured it untouched down the bathroom sink, feeling very noble as she did so. She found herself a little short-tempered later in the evening, a little edgy, but that was simply because she had gotten into the habit of relaxing with a drink and she missed it. But it was no real need on her part, for goodness sake.

The next day at noon she started to go to the corner hamburger heaven. If she wasn't going to have a drink, there was no point in going to a good restaurant. Wait, she thought—why be so silly? She could certainly enjoy a good meal at a good restaurant without a drink. A drink might improve the meal, but it was hardly necessary. In any case, she was hungry, and she could use a good lunch.

That afternoon she messed up two phone calls, something she rarely did. Her typing was terrible—Gordon gave her only one letter to do, and she had to do it four times before she came up with presentable copy. By the time she left the office her head was splitting and the roof of her mouth was bone-dry.

I don't need it, she told herself. It's not that I *need* a drink. Just that I feel rotten, and I would feel a good deal better with a drink, and there was surely no point in this silly little test anyway. It was nonsense, pure nonsense. It didn't mean a thing.

What was it all about, anyway? Mortifying the flesh like a repentant sinner? Undergoing some foolishly symbolic martyrdom like a psychotic bucking for sainthood?

Silly.

She went straight from the office to a small bar on 45th Street near Madison. She sat at the bar—something she had never done before—and she knocked off three straight Scotches. Miraculously, the headache went away, the tension disappeared, the nerves calmed down.

It didn't mean a thing she told herself.

But she didn't believe it at all.

Chapter 9

The three drinks had hit her hard. She took a cab home and felt slightly rocky in the back seat. She sat up straight, gripped the seat in front of her with both hands as if this would make her stomach calm down.

"Something wrong, Miss?"

"No," she said. "Nothing's wrong."

But she made the cab driver stop the car on the corner of Third Avenue, and she paid and dismissed him and stood on the corner for a few moments gulping air. It didn't mean a thing, she told herself, but she knew better than to believe that convenient lie. She thought of going home, to Rae, and she hesitated. Of course Rae didn't know about her little test, and would not know that she had failed, but, still, she couldn't bring herself to go to the apartment and face the blonde girl. She had been drinking—not because she wanted to but because she had to. This bothered her, and it kept her from going to the apartment.

Instead, she went to a bar. A bar on the corner of Third Avenue, a neighborhood pub with half a dozen men in it and no women at all. She sat at the bar and the men stared at her. She half-hoped one of them would approach her so that she could tell him what he could do to himself. No one did. The bartender came, and that was what she really wanted, of course.

"Double Scotch," she said . . .

⤙•⤚

She had never been this drunk before. She could still get around perfectly well, could walk straight, could manage to navigate. And her mind seemed to be working with perfect clarity. Nevertheless, she was rotten drunk and she knew it.

When she opened the apartment door Rae got up out of the chair and started toward her. "Oh, my god," she was saying. "Baby, I was worried sick about you. Do you know what time it is? Why didn't you call? What happened to you? Where *were* you, for godssake?"

"Sorry."

"Sorry! Oh, you're drunk, Karen, what on earth is wrong with you? I don't understand it, baby. What on earth—"

"You don't own me, Rae."

The blonde girl stepped back as if she had been slapped brutally across the face. Her hand came up in defensive reflex. Her mouth fell open.

"Karen . . ."

"I'm a big girl now," she heard herself say, "I can do what I damn well want."

"But—"

"You want to know something? You're turning into a nag."

"You don't know what you're saying."

"Don't I? Let go of me."

"You'd better go to sleep now, Karen."

"Damn it, you're not my mother."

She couldn't believe what was happening, could not understand what she herself was doing. It was crazy—she was fighting with Rae, making nothing at all into a horrible fight, and she was conscious of what she was doing but couldn't do a thing to stop it. It was almost schizophrenic, as if there were two Karens and she was sitting across the room, helpless to interfere, while one of her was making a mess out of everything.

And she shouted at Rae, accused her of jealousy, railed at her, cut her with words sharper than knives.

"I'll do what I want, do you understand me? If I want to have a drink I'll have one, do you hear me? I can go where I want and do what I please, I didn't start sleeping with you because I wanted some yellow-haired tramp to mother me, do you hear me?"

Rae heard her. The whole neighborhood could have heard her; she was shouting at the top of her lungs.

"Karen, you don't know what you're saying."

"The hell I don't."

"Karen, baby, what did I *do*? What's the matter?"

"Everything's the matter."

"Karen! Karen, where are you going? Oh, don't leave now. Don't leave me. Karen, don't! Not the way you feel now. You'll hurt yourself, you'll hurt us both. Stay, baby. I'll make you a cup of tea."

"I don't want any."

"Then coffee. Anything, Karen, calm down, don't leave now, not in the shape you're in. Baby, you'll hurt yourself, you'll get in awful trouble."

"Get out of my way."

"Karen!"

"Get out of my way!"

She stormed out the door, shoved her way past Rae. The blonde girl was crying now, helpless.

"When will you be back? Karen, honey—"

"Shut up!"

~⌐•⌐~

She never remembered how she got downtown. She probably took a cab, but she remembered nothing between the time when she stormed out of the apartment and the time she was standing in a dirty basement bar on a quiet street in the lower section of the Village. She wasn't sure of the name of the street and never knew how she had found the place. It seemed inconceivable that she could have located the bar by mere accident, since it was off the beaten track and she had never before been aware of its existence. Perhaps she had simply asked the cabdriver (if she took a cab) to take her to a lesbian hang-out. That seemed unlikely enough, but there was no other logical explanation for her having turned up there.

It was not a pleasant place. A juke box gave out with harsh gut-bucket blues. A long bar ran the length of the narrow room, and a handful of tables were scattered along the opposite wall. The tables were mostly empty. The bar itself was jammed. She had to wedge her way up to it, and had to wait for awhile before a broad-shouldered short-haired girl came over to take her order. She ordered a double shot of Scotch with a water chaser and drank it off as soon as it came.

The bar was a lesbian place. There was not a man in it, although some of the female customers were mannish enough to fool you unless you looked rather closely at them. She stood at the bar with the Scotch burning its way into her system and she sipped the water chaser and felt suddenly very much alone, lost in the middle of a crowd. She told herself that she should not feel alone, not here of all places. After all, she was with her own kind.

A wave of remorse washed over her. She thought of what she had said and done to Rae and she wanted to cry, to scream. It was wrong, all wrong, it had been her fault entirely, and she could not understand what made her act as she had acted. She should be home right now, she told herself. She should be home with Rae, and instead she was at this stupid ugly foul bar and no one was even paying any attention to her and she should be ashamed of herself, horribly and dreadfully ashamed of herself . . .

There was a spell of blankness. The next thing that impressed itself upon her memory was when she found herself dancing with a tall, heavyset butch with short black hair and a chin pitted with acne scars. The music was slow and suggestive and the butch smelled incredibly of a combination of sweat and man's aftershave lotion. The heavy girl was holding her tightly in her arms. Karen felt the girl's body brush against her own breasts, felt the insinuating probe of the butch's loins against her own. She was at once repelled and excited. It was all very sickening, and at the same time a quiver of naked lust shot through her, jabbing her almost painfully in breasts and groin, stirring her in an astonishing way.

The girl was whispering in her ear: "Baby, let's get out of here, you and me, huh? You got a place we can go to? I got a pad but my chick is there, you know, and I got no eyes to see her tonight. Baby, we'll go some place, you and me, I'll do things you never did, I'll show you scenes you never dreamed about, baby . . ."

Consciousness drifted in and out, dipped and faded. She kept on drinking. Memories rushed back and forth in shreds and patches of light among the darkness.

Memories: Dancing in a corner, a dark corner with some other girl, a slender doll-faced slip of a girl. The girl was moaning softly. Karen had her hand up beneath the girl's skirt. The girl writhed in her grasp as she probed with urgent fingers, found, touched, caressed.

Memories: Sitting at a table, crying, crying desperately. One girl wanting to know what was wrong, another girl saying *Leave her alone, let her be, the kid's got things to cry about, give her air and leave her alone.*

Memories: Another bar, quieter, more refined. She sat at a table with a butch who had a hand on her leg and a girl passed and looked at her, and she looked up at the girl and recognized her. A tall over-blown blonde, an exotic dancer, one of Leon Gordon's clients. The girl had been in and out of the agent's office two and three times a week, and Karen had never expected to see her in a place like this. The girl—she couldn't remember her name— was saying, "Well, I'll be damned! Hi, honey—I never knew you were one of the girls. I would have said hello nicer if I knew. One of these days, honey lover girl . . ."

Memories: Walking through black streets arm in arm with a mannish girl, smoking cigarettes, weaving drunkenly from side to side. The butch's arm around her waist, a hand drifting up to cup her breasts, a voice in her ear . . .

Then, for a while, no more memories.

❧•❧

She woke brutally, her head splitting, her stomach churning, a furious pain in her tender loins. She did not know where she was. She looked around and saw a room she had never seen before, and all at once it was like waking up in that hospital after her attempt at suicide; once again she did not know where she was or how she had gotten there. Now she was not alone. There was someone beside her, the butch she had walked the streets with. The girl was older than she, Karen saw. She was sleeping on her side, facing Karen, her mouth slack, breathing heavily. She was a heavyish woman in her late thirties, with pancake breasts and muscular thighs and a cruel mouth, even when it was relaxed in sleep.

She tore her eyes from the butch, and she stumbled to her feet and dashed for the door. It led not to the bathroom, as she had hoped, but to a closet, and she collapsed against the door frame and vomited into a slovenly pile of coats and dresses.

The butch slept on. Karen looked at her again, looked unwillingly at the girl with whom she had made love. She must have been unconscious, she told herself. She must have passed out, and then the rotten dyke must have raped her while she was too drunk to know what was happening.

Or else . . .

Or else she had been aware of what was going on. Or else she had participated, had actually enjoyed it all and responded to it all, taking some ungodly pleasure from the horror of the embrace. It was too horrid to think of it that way, and once again her stomach turned at the image of what had been done to her and what she must have done, how she must have acted, what she might have said and done and all, all of it too much to bear.

She couldn't stay there, not for another moment. She could not bear the thought of spending another minute in that room. And she did not know what would happen if the butch awakened. What could she do? What would she say?

In a panic, she got into her clothes and tore out of the room and down flight after flight of stairs to the street below. She hurried through the cold yellow light of dawn, not knowing where she was or where she was going, only anxious to get as far away from the scene of last night's disgrace as she could.

At last she stopped. She went into a luncheonette and forced herself to have a cup of coffee. She bought aspirin at a drugstore and had the clerk bring her a glass of water. Her headache gradually receded, her stomach finally began to calm down. It had miles to go, but it was better.

She took a cab home. Not because she wanted to, not because she honestly thought she could face Rae. But because she had to see the blonde girl, had to find some way to wipe the slate at least part of the way clean.

But how? And what was she supposed to do now? What would she say? Worse, what would let her get through the day, and the next day, and the one after that?

She looked at her watch. It was almost seven, which meant that she was due at the office in a little over two hours. She didn't think she could make it. She looked like hell and felt worse, and she knew it wouldn't do her an awful lot of good to put in eight hours behind a desk. Nor would it do Mr. Gordon any good. He had told her that her job was to look pretty, to lend the office a note of what he called class. And she did not feel, somehow, that she could lend class to anything; the way she looked and felt, she would reduce the appearance of an outhouse.

When the cab stopped, when she dragged herself into the

apartment, she was not tremendously surprised to find that Rae had left. It was logical enough. She had come home late and drunk, and she had been completely rotten in every way saying unforgivable things and doing unforgivable things, and of course Rae had left.

There was a note:

Karen—

I don't know what's the matter but I do know that I can't possibly stay here now. I tried to tell myself that the drinking was just a phase and thought you would get through it but we both know better than that now. And tonight was too much, maybe it's my fault for being weak but I can't and won't go through that sort of scene. I've had it before and I won't have it again.

I'll be staying at a hotel for a little while. I think we need a chance to settle down, and you need time to decide what's what. I'll be in touch.

I still love you, and always will, I fear.

Your Rae

At nine o'clock she called Gordon's office and no one answered the phone. She smoked two cigarettes and tried him again. "This is Karen," she said. "I'm not feeling well, Mister Gordon. I don't think I can come in today."

"Sure, kid. You take care of yourself. Figure you'll be out any length of time?"

"I don't think so. But if I spend a day in bed . . ."

"You do that, Karen. Just take things easy until you feel a little better, okay?"

It was not a lie, she thought as she put the receiver back in its cradle. She was definitely not feeling well, and she definitely couldn't come in that day. And she would spend the day in bed, just as soon as she got herself fixed properly so that she would be able to sleep again.

The boy from the liquor store delivered a quart of Johnny Walker Red Label.

She took one small drink, then got out of her clothes and went into the bathroom. She spent a long time under the shower, scrubbing the scent and taste of sick lust from her skin. She washed herself again and again, as if her entire body were as imbued with the essence of depravity as Lady Macbeth's uncleansable hand. *Here's the taste of lust still, all the perfumes of Arabia will not sweeten this little girl...*

She left the shower at last and toweled herself dry. Then she took the bottle of Scotch and crawled into her bed—*their* bed, she thought—and drank until she was able to slip securely off to sleep.

Chapter 10

Her fingers curled around the stem of the glass on the table before her. She drew a breath, let it out slowly, and raised the glass to her lips. She took one small sip and put it down before her. One drink with lunch—that was the system she had decided upon. One drink and no more with lunch, and then nothing until she had finished work for the day. Then back to the apartment, back to the awful loneliness of the apartment, and one drink before dinner, and then . . .

Then she would drink herself to sleep. But no heavy boozing before then. One drink at lunch to take the edge off, one drink with dinner to give the food some flavor. After dinner, home, alone, so desperately alone, she could drink herself into a stupor with a clear conscience.

"You're looking dreadfully sad today," Adrian March said.

"Am I?" She smiled. "I'm sorry."

"Is something wrong, Karen?"

"Oh not really. A . . . a good friend of mine whom I used to see . . . someone I used to see rather often . . . well, moved away for the time being, you see, and I'm a little blue. Nothing I won't get over."

She wondered how true that was, wondered if there was any

chance that Rae would come back. One night Rae *had* come back, and that could have been her chance, and she blew it to hell and gone. It had been a desperate night, and after she had carefully limited herself to that single drink at lunch and that solitary cocktail before dinner, she had gone back to the apartment and really hung one on.

And, when she was about ten seconds away from the neutral blessing of unconsciousness, Rae walked in.

So that tore it.

If she had been sober, they would have kissed and made up. But she was not remotely sober, was in fact about as far as it was possible to be from sobriety, and they did not come close to making up. She tried. She did a great deal of crying and begging and promising and more crying, and Rae sobbed some, and Rae wound up filling another of her suitcases and walking out the door. She would be out of town for awhile, the blonde girl explained. It would give them both a chance to cool off a little. And when she came back, in two or three weeks, or maybe a month . . .

"A boyfriend, Karen?"

She started. March was smiling gently, and she drew herself quickly back to the conversation. No, she thought. A girlfriend, whom I love, who used to sleep with me.

"Yes," she said. "A boyfriend."

Because what point was there in telling him embarrassing things, things he did not need to know?

"He'll come back."

"Maybe he will. And maybe not."

"He will if he knows what he's about."

She forced a smile. "You're sweet," she said.

When the office door opened she turned on the intercom and said, "Oh, hello, Miss Jones. Can I help you?"

I'll see her, Gordon's signal flashed.

The dancer smiled hugely, and in that instant Karen remembered. Cherry Jones was the girl she had seen on that horrid lost night in the Village. At the lesbian bar.

Hastily she flicked the switch to cut off the intercom, just as Cherry Jones said, "Look who's here! Little Miss Lovely—"

She gasped for breath. "I—"

"Don't be embarrassed, baby. I've been a long time thinking about you, you dig? Funny the way you don't tune in on people you see all the time. Like part of the furniture. I saw you here all those times and I never guessed you were a swinger."

The dancer wore too much makeup. Karen saw her breasts were almost absurdly large, all out of proportion. Her dress was cut far too low in the front and was far too tight around her opulent hips. And, beneath the makeup, her face was harsh, tough, not pretty at all. And yet, in spite of this, she felt an unwelcome stirring in her loins, an unwanted quiver of desire.

She had never felt this rush of heady hunger for a girl other than Rae. Not when she was sober, at any rate. On that night in the Village everything had been twisted all out of proportion and she could scarcely recall what she *felt*; it was bad enough that she remembered a portion of what she *did* and a portion of what was done to her.

But now . . .

"Mister Gordon will see you now," she stammered.

"He can wait a minute, Karen. That's your name, isn't it? Karen?"

She nodded.

"And you're all strung out because somebody knows your secret. Don't let it hang you up. You know my secret, too, don't you? And I don't exactly run ads in *Billboard* telling the world that I like the girls just as much as the men like me. See?"

She didn't say anything. If only she didn't find this girl so overwhelmingly attractive, she thought, then she might be able to hold up her end of the conversation. And yet she wanted the stripper and disliked her at the same time. It was not a healthy attraction. It was purely sexual, a physical longing that made her enormously uncomfortable.

"We ought to get together, Karen."

"I don't—"

"I'm not all-the-way gay, you know. I swing . . . both ways, is what I mean. Boys or girls. Whatever rings the bell. I've got a long feeling we could ring a couple or three bells for each other, doll. See?"

"I—"

"I'd better see Leon now. Sit tight, little doll."

While the stripper was in Gordon's office she buzzed him on the phone. "I've got a yen for a cup of coffee," she said. "Okay if I duck out for a minute or two?"

"Sure thing," he said. "Bring me back a coffee and Danish, will you?"

She took her time, hoping the stripper would be gone when she returned. She dawdled at the lunch counter and thought about the girl. That would be the end of the whole thing, she told herself. A cheap brazen tramp named Cherry Jones. A girl who could come up with such gems as *I swing both ways. Boys or girls. Whatever rings the bell . . .*

When she got back to the office the stripper had already left. She said a silent prayer of thanks, took Gordon his coffee and Danish pastry, then returned to her desk. There was a small business card on her desk near the telephone. It was scented with some sort of musky perfume.

Black raised lettering on a pale green card.

And, on an upward slant, the girl had written: *Call me when you're in the mood.*

Don't hold your breath, Karen thought. Don't hold your goddamned breath.

But three nights later, three Rae-less nights later, alone, so badly alone, so entirely alone, she put down the bottle and padded over to the telephone and dialed a number.

I should have died long ago, she thought, hating herself, hating the world. I should have bled to death on Rivington Street. I would have been better off that way.

And, when a familiar voice answered, she said, "I'm in the mood, Miss Cherry Ice-Cream-Soda Jones. I'm in the mood."

Chapter 11

The bottle was empty by the time her doorbell sounded. She walked carefully to the door, placing one foot very precisely before the other, very pleased to discover that she was capable of walking the straightest of lines drunk or not. And tonight she knew that it was very good to be drunk. Tonight sobriety was unthinkable. When you took a trip to Hell, you had to bring your camera.

Darling forgive me, she prayed silently, for I know not what I do . . .

When she opened the door she saw two women standing in the hallway. Cherry was there, dressed almost obscenely in the tightest slacks she had ever seen and a gold lamé sweater that covered her like a coat of sparkling paint. And, next to Cherry, she saw a very thin slip of a girl with a long equine face and washed-out blondish hair worn in a pony tail. The girl smiled and showed large teeth.

"I brought a friend," Cherry said. "Hope you don't mind."

"I—"

"After all," the stripper said, "any number can play. The rules of the game are flexible, doll."

She didn't know what to say. She stepped aside, and Cherry and the other girl came into the apartment. The girl could not have been more than eighteen, Karen thought. If that. She wore a paisley shirt with a button-down collar and a pair of black flannel slacks. Her wrists were very thin, with a tracery of blue veins showing prominently. Her eyes, Karen saw, had a glint in them that was almost psychopathic.

"This is Evelyn," Cherry said. "A protégée, so to speak. Ev, doll, this is Karen, receptionist and Gal Tuesday for the illustrious Leon Gordon, purveyor of human flesh." Cherry flashed a smile. "Why don't you two kiss hello?"

Karen did not believe that this was happening. No lovemaking could be so utterly lacking in feeling, so wholly devoid of anything but the elements of desire. The slender girl came toward her and raised her pale lips for a kiss, and Karen found herself kissing the upturned mouth while she marveled at her own apparently limitless capacity for depravity. Because this was entirely depraved and she could not believe it was actually happening, that she was actually letting herself get involved in something so extraordinary. This would pass, she knew. In a moment or two this ephemeral illusion of sobriety would fade out and the alcohol in her bloodstream would take control, and she would be able to relax and enjoy it all.

And that, somehow, was the most frightening aspect of the whole affair.

"Got anything to drink, Karen?"

"No."

"Guess you worked your way through all the juice before you called. Dutch courage, sugar?"

"Maybe."

"People get themselves in such a state. Life's too short to get all hung up on things. No point. Something's fun, you go ahead and do it. Something looks like a groove, you see if it lives up to expectations. Spend a lot of time thinking and all you do is buy yourself a headache." Cherry looked to the thin young girl for confirmation. "Am I right, Ev?"

"The rightest," Evelyn said. It was the first she had spoken. Her eyes danced and her head bobbed in time to some imaginary tune audible only to her. Her voice was low, throaty, bubbling. She sighed lazily and her hands reached boldly out, to grasp Karen at the waist. "Crazy, crazy," she said, and Karen felt a spasm of desire strike her in the chest with the force of a coronary explosion. She fell forward into the girl's arms and sought her pale lips greedily, and the girl kissed her and laughed and kissed her again. Karen closed her eyes and surrendered to the kiss. She could hear Evelyn's rapid breathing, could hear Cherry taking off her clothes, then padding nude about the room to turn off all of the lights but one.

Cherry whispered, "Don't be selfish, dear." And Evelyn giggled softly, her laughter like ice cubes in a tall drink, and she kissed Karen a final time and rubbed their bodies together and then released her. Karen swayed on her feet, at the point of collapse. Then the tall stripper took her into her arms, and she was pressed against Cherry's nude and opulent body from head to toe. She felt the weight and warmth of the dancer's huge breasts, the heat of her loins, the strength of her tightly muscled arms and legs.

A kiss . . .

She felt as though she were being passed back and forth, like a wine bottle shared amongst congenial alcoholics in a Bowery hallway. And, responding to the force and fever of Cherry's embrace, she felt again like two people in one body, the one observing, the other participating—the one disapproving, the other too caught up in desire to care. The Two-Karens Syndrome, she thought. And then she stopped thinking entirely and let the second Karen take over completely . . .

~•~

Brittle visions.

A beach by night. High tide and a haze around the moon. A wash of furious surf on the sea, waves dashing against a break wall, rolling onto the sand.

Lightning splitting the opaque face of the sky. Stark silence, and then the rumble and roll of thunder out over the sea. Silence once more, and a girl's shriek rending the sheer fabric of the night.

Upon the sound, a rattle and a hiss. A diamondback rattlesnake, eyes like chips of agate, tongue flashing in a burlesque of forbidden lust, head back, body coiled in desperation, poised to strike. A rattle, a hiss, the snake's body thrusting out straight and firm and rather like a man.

Waves high as housetops, waves that did not break, waves that towered up onto the beach, up over the sand, up over the snake and the shrieking girl, high, wide, as wet as death, as wet as blood.

Brittle visions, dark as drowning, close as Hell.

~•~

The bed, once hers and Rae's, then hers alone, had seemed impossibly large when she had slept in it by herself—oceans of mattress on every side, deserts of empty space all around her.

Now, as she betrayed both Rae and herself in that bed, it seemed strangely small. A little bed overfilled with female flesh in abject abandon.

She lay on her back holding Evelyn in her arms while Cherry was kissing her legs. She held Evelyn's little breasts and squeezed them. Like tiny teacups without handles, like the little cups of green tea they served at Chinese restaurants. Almost tasteless tea until you learned to breathe its fragrance, and then it went to your head and delighted you . . .

A rolling peal of laughter from the girl. Insane, Karen thought. A literally insane person, over the edge of the mind's bright eye, out of touch with the serrated edge of reality.

But who was she to judge insanity? To cast stones through the walls of her own glass castle? To build fires in the halls of her own private ice palace?

Bodies moved upon the bed. There ought to be more liquor, she thought. More alcohol to fasten once and for all the doors of perception, to shut them and bar them permanently. This was bad, this occasional spasm of the conscience. Another few drinks and she would have shut out the perceptive Karen entirely; a few less drinks and she would have spent the evening alone instead of having her flesh shared by these two lovely devils.

Watch out for Mister In-Between . . .

Evelyn's face danced before her. The girl's eyes flashed fire, cold fire. and the girl's tongue darted out and it was the snake's tongue, forked like a devil's tail, and Evelyn's head weaved and bobbed like the rattlesnake readying to strike, and Karen's ears screamed with a rattle and a hiss and a shriek in the stillness of the night.

"Oh, you're evil," she said aloud. "That's what you are, did you know? Cold fire. Evil."

A roar of laughter. Glass shattering. Someone—Cherry?—singing an old Eartha Kitt song. *I want to be evil, I want to be bad . . .*

When did it end, how did it end? And where? It seemed now to be endless. Some of the time the perceptive Karen withered and died, and she entered into the spirit of lust with complete abandon and nothing held back, nothing in reserve. Other times she did not know what she did because the memory failed to register. And other times a thread, a ribbon, a trace of perception returned and imposed itself upon her. But still the endless parade endured, still the bodies tumbled in the bed, still lips and tongues and fingers and breasts and thighs and loins played the endless game in endless pointless mindless soulless hunger.

During one of the moments of awareness she lipped a silent prayer. A small request, one God could grant with no effort at all. Sooner or later, she knew, it would have to end. Sooner or later she or they or all of them would pass out. Sooner or later the blackness of sleep would roll in like fog.

And sooner or later after that she would awaken.

Her prayer was not elaborate. She only wished that, when she did awake, they would be gone and she would be alone. Just that much.

Chapter 12

"Mister Gordon? This is Karen. I'm afraid I won't be coming in to-day, Mister Gordon, I . . . I'm going to have to have some time off. I'm not sure how long. A few weeks, maybe. I don't really know how much time."

He wanted to know what was wrong.

"Everything's wrong," she said. She looked down at the palm of her hand. It was beaded with perspiration. She wiped her palm on her slacks, transferred the phone to that hand, wiped the sweat from her other hand.

"Kid, is it money? Because I could help."

"It's not money," she said. "Everything's a mess, I don't know what I'm going to do. I suppose I ought to get out of this city but I wouldn't know where to go. I feel as though I'm all tied up in knots and I have to get loose before I strangle." She hadn't meant to run on like this but once she'd started it was impossible to stop. Her hand tightened on the telephone receiver as if she were trying to squeeze water from it. "I don't know what I'm going to do next, I'm all messed up and I don't know what to do. I thought everything was all straightened out, and I thought I was doing fine, just fine, and I love working for you and everything else, and—"

She stopped cold in the middle of the sentence, slapped a lid on the flow of words. "I'm sorry," she said. "I didn't mean to carry on like a two-year-old. I don't know when I'll be able to come back to the office, Mister Gordon. Maybe you ought to hire another girl. All I can say is that I'd like to come back when this is all straightened out but I don't know when that will be and in the meanwhile I couldn't possibly work. I'm having enough trouble just trying to keep from snapping inside."

"Karen?"

"Yes?"

There was a pause while he hunted for the words. Then he said, "I don't like this talk about finding somebody else. You're perfect for what I want, you've always done perfect work. You're what the office needs, honey."

In spite of everything, his words meant something to her. All at once there was a lump in her throat, a mass in her chest pressing against her rib cage. In another minute, she thought, I'll start to cry.

"So get off this kick of hire-somebody-else. All these years in the business I ran my office by myself, the hell, I can do it again until you're ready to come back. In a week or three weeks or three months. I know how to pick up a phone, for godsake, I know how to dodge somebody I don't want to see. I'll put the answering service on full-time the way it used to be and I'll manage. Don't think I won't miss you, but I'll manage, I'll wait for you."

She thought, *What a sweet man, what an impossibly sweet man.*

"Listen to me," he went on. "This is all none of my business, so you tell me to go to hell if you want, all right? But a lot of the time a young kid thinks she's got a problem that nobody ever had before, and most of the problems in the world have been around a long time. And somebody who's fifty can see that the problems people have at twenty aren't as rough as they seem at the time. Listen to the old philosopher, huh?"

She found she was almost smiling.

"Karen, tell me, are you pregnant?" He was talking very swiftly now, as if embarrassed by his own question. "Because every girl thinks that's the end of the world, and believe me, it never is. There are doctors who take care of that kind of thing, good doctors, not two-bit rabbit snatchers but good professional expensive Park Avenue doctors who do the whole bit in regular hospital conditions so that nothing goes wrong. Or there are places you can go where nobody looks at you funny and you wait your time and when you're through you've had the kid and it goes straight out for adoption, you never even see it and you know it winds up in a good home, and nobody knows where you were, you were just out of town on a vacation and you never had a baby at all. Or if you want to marry the sonofabitch there are ways to arrange that, too, and it's not as hard as you think and not as easy for him to get out of marrying you as maybe he thinks it is. What I'm trying to say, and I know it's none of my business, but the point is that it's not as bad as you maybe think it is, and you don't have to worry about money for a doctor or a place to stay or anything, because that can all be taken care of and no strings. What Sophie Tucker says, *I've been rich and I've been poor and rich is better,* well the best thing about having a couple of bucks is you can help somebody when she needs help, so don't you worry about the money."

He stopped, breathless, and she discovered that she *was* crying.

It didn't surprise her. She swallowed and got control of herself. She said, "You would do all that for me?"

"Sure."

"Why?"

A pause. Then, with a verbal shrug, "Well, you're a nice kid, Karen. You've been a real help around the office. The hell . . ."

She thought how very extraordinary everything was. If she had been working for this so-sweet man when she had been pregnant with Ronnie's child, if she had known someone like him or Adrian March, then she would never have wound up in that cold empty room on Rivington Street, would never have drawn red lines on her wrists with a razor blade. How wonderful some people could be, she thought. How very wonderful some people could be.

And she told him, then, that she was not pregnant. Almost cheerfully she said, "I wish it were only that. It's not anything concrete that I can point to. It's . . . all inside, the way I've been feeling and acting, the general way my life is going. I need time to think. I have to figure out what's happening to me. I'm all mixed up, half the time I can't think straight. The whole thing . . . I wish it was something another person could help with but I don't think it is. I think it's the sort of thing I have to work out by myself."

"Would you want to see a doctor?"

"I don't think so."

"Don't take this the wrong way, but what I meant was a psychiatrist. I don't know if they do anybody any good but some people swear by them. The others swear *at* them. It might be worth trying, Karen."

She had thought of this before. Maybe she was wrong, but she couldn't believe that a psychiatrist or psychoanalyst could help her.

She had the certain feeling that whatever had to be done was something she had to do entirely alone, and that she had to find her own way through the woods.

"Anything I can do, honey, anything at all, you know enough to come to me, I hope."

"I know."

"Money, a shoulder to cry on, a ticket to some other town. Anything, you let me know. You don't and I'll be insulted."

She couldn't speak.

"And whenever you're ready, just walk through the door. The job'll be there for you whenever it is. Don't be in any rush. Get everything out of your system. Take your time. You mind another question? Would you get upset if you got your weekly check in the mail while you're out?"

"Please don't do that."

"You could call it a loan if you wanted. Or an advance against future salary."

"No, please." She swallowed again. "I'd honestly rather not."

"You all right financially?"

"I've got some money set aside. It'll be enough."

"Okay, it's your business, but the offer always stands. There's something else. You can collect unemployment insurance. It's something you paid for, it's not charity, they deduct out of your pay every week and you might as well get some good out of it. You apply, and when they check with me I'll say I let you go because I found out I didn't need a girl and couldn't afford the salary. That way you'll be eligible to collect. Will you do that much?"

"I don't know."

"You damn well ought to, you paid money in, why not get some benefit from it? You get thirty-five or forty bucks a week, tax-free, something like that. And it's not charity. Do me a favor and go down to the unemployment place later this week and apply. Will you promise to do that?"

"All right."

"Good, good." He was silent. "Well," he said, "I guess that's it, huh? Take care of yourself. And this is very soap opera, but it's never as bad as it seems. Nothing ever is. Soap opera or not, it's the truth. You remember that?"

"I'll remember," she said.

Not that day but the following afternoon Rae called. She knew the phone would ring sooner or later and she had been sitting patiently waiting for the call. She was very calm when she answered it.

"I hoped we'd both had a chance to relax," Rae said. "I wanted to find out where we stand."

"I think we should see each other."

"Shall I come over?"

"No, I don't think so." She lit a cigarette. "Rae, I'm going to have to move out of the apartment for awhile. There are a lot of things I have to figure out for myself. I can't even put everything in words right now but I need some time alone."

"Stay in the apartment. I'm comfortable where I am."

"No. No, I have to get away. Oh, this is impossible, isn't it? I want to talk to you face to face. Can you meet me some place?"

"Neutral territory?"

"You could call it that. Where can I meet you?" Rae named a cocktail lounge.

"No, not there. Some place for coffee. The Ham 'n' Eggs on Union Square? Is that all right with you?"

"Not a bar? That's a change."

"Yes. I . . . Could you meet me at the Ham 'n' Eggs in half an hour?"

"I'll be there, Karen."

And, in a back booth where they faced each other over a Formica-topped table, she drank coffee and chain-smoked and tried to explain what she had to do and how she thought that she felt. It was a very difficult conversation. Rae wanted to know if there was someone else, if Karen still loved her, if she had done something too horribly wrong. The blonde girl began to berate herself for having moved out, for having been inconsiderate when Karen needed her.

"You were all messed up and I turned into a perfect bitch. My god, Karen, you must hate me!"

"No," she said. She wanted to say more but couldn't.

"Do you think . . . do you—"

"I can't really talk now," she said.

"You're right. Oh, the awful things people do to each other. And to themselves."

She ground out a cigarette, lit another almost immediately. "I'll pack my things and be moved out by this evening, Rae. You can move in tonight or tomorrow morning."

"Are you leaving some of your things, Karen?"

"No, I don't think so."

"You're packing everything, kitten? Then that means you're not coming back, doesn't it?"

She blew out a column of smoke. "I honestly don't know," she said. "I . . . just don't know, that's all. That's one of the things I have to work out for myself."

"Do you mean that? Or is this just a handy way to let me down gently? Because you don't have to be gentle with me, kitten, I've made this scene too many times already to need the kid-glove treatment. Nothing ever lasts in our world. I told you that at the beginning, didn't I? *Always is a lie.* And my kitten will never come back to me. Will she?"

"I—I—I—" She was stuttering, absolutely unable to make the words take form. She stopped and closed her eyes and forced herself to sit back in the booth. Her hands knotted themselves into fists, relaxed, knotted up again. Finally she said again that she didn't know what she was going to do, that she might not go back to Rae, that she might return later if Rae still wanted her, that she just honestly didn't know.

"You'd better go now," Rae said.

She didn't say anything.

"Leave the restaurant. Now. Please. Just leave, I'll take care of the check. I love you, Karen. *Please* go, I'm going to cry. I don't want you to see me, please go, darling . . ."

It was hard to find a hotel; there were very few neighborhoods left for her. The Upper West Side was where she had lived with Ronnie, the Lower East Side was where she had attempted to kill herself, the Gramercy Park section was where she had lived with Rae, and the Village was where she had gone off the deep end. It seemed as though every corner of Manhattan was a web of yet another set of memories she was anxious to escape. There were neighborhoods where she had not lived, neighborhoods she did not know at all, but they did not seem to have hotels in them.

She thought how extraordinary it would sound if she ever tried to explain her dilemma to anyone. Sooner or later, she thought, the March Hare and the Mad Hatter and the Dormouse had to work their way around even the longest of tables, until at last every place was messed. Sooner or later one had to have bad memories of every section of a city, until there was no place left for one to live in.

Just to get away. Just to go far enough so that she would never see anyone she knew, never pass any place she had ever been. And yet she wanted to remain in New York. She did not want to leave the city. She had never been out of the area in her life, and she sure she would be utterly lost anywhere else.

The hotel she ultimately chose was not in Manhattan but deep in Brooklyn on Flatbush Avenue near Eastern Parkway. She remembered the Thomas Wolfe story . . . Only the dead knew Brooklyn, according to the title, and this seemed somehow appropriate. She was dead, in a very real sense, and she wanted a chance to find a way to live again, and to find it in a place she did not know and a place where no one would know her.

The hotel was called the Rainier Arms. It was shabby but clean and seemed monotonously proper. The other guests, as well as she could gather, were pensioners and widows and widowers, tired old people who wanted a clean and respectable place with minimal up-keep and no lease to sign while they tried to make their low incomes and small savings cover the years it took them to get around to dying. It was just the sort of place she wanted, close to wherever she wanted to go yet impossibly remote in that she could live there forever and never encounter anyone from her past life in Manhattan. And her fellow-tenants were perfect—there was not a single one she had the slightest interest in speaking with, and they seemed equally inclined to leave her alone while their arteries hardened. Her room was neat, sparsely but adequately furnished, flooded with sunlight from two to five in the afternoon when the sun managed to get through between the taller buildings. The hotel service was there if she needed it. Her bed was made every morning, towels furnished, linens changed weekly. She could place or receive telephone calls through the hotel switchboard, and they would take messages for her while she was out. This was a service she would not use, she knew; no one knew where she was staying, and there was no one she intended to call. She did not even bother checking for mail at the hotel desk. She knew the only sort of mail she might receive—soap coupons addressed to *Occupant*, letters from her Congressman (whoever he might be), charity appeals.

The neighborhood itself had all the conveniences she could conceivably require. There was a shopping section on Flatbush, a movie theater down the street, a library just two blocks away. She had to go into Manhattan periodically to pick up her unemployment checks, her one major concession to Leon Gordon. She had registered for unemployment, and she had listed her job not as *receptionist* but as *theatrical agent*, a slight lie which Gordon had backed. Since no one ever told the state employment service he was looking to hire a theatrical agent, they had no cause to send her out for job interviews. They simply paid her thirty-seven dollars and seventy-five cents a week and left her alone.

Her hotel rent was ten dollars and seventy cents a week, an unusual but reasonable sum. By making instant coffee on a hotplate in her room and scrimping generally on meals, she found that she could live on her weekly stipend with very little difficulty. She didn't even have to touch her savings, and she was glad of that. Although she had sounded secure enough when she talked to Gordon, she had very little money set aside.

In a sense she realized, she was back where she had been when they discharged her from the hospital. The two situations had several points in common—a new neighborhood, a furnished room, no job, no personal contacts, and scars that had to heal. This time all of the scars were inside. Her wrists were unscathed. And this time, instead of being content to let the days go by at their own pace, instead of living one day at a time, instead of hating her loneliness and filling time until she could start work and find a friend, she had to take an active role in straightening herself out.

Because otherwise she would be in trouble.

In bad trouble, she knew. She was at a fork in the road, and the fork had many branches. One led to a nervous breakdown and confinement in a mental hospital. Another led to the living death of alcoholism. A third pointed to an ever-deeper spiral of sexual depravity and self-loathing. A fourth was a road she had tried to take once before—self-murder, suicide. But she was sure that there was at least one other course open, one other road for her to take, one that would lead her out of the shadows and into the sunshine, one that would take her where she could live again.

No one could find the road for her. She knew this with complete assurance. If it was there—and if it wasn't she was lost, lost, as good as dead—but if it was there, she knew that she would have to find it herself.

So she needed a system, a regimen. She needed not the peace and quiet and aimless haphazard drifting she had tried upon leaving the hospital, but required instead something entirely different, the utter opposite.

She had to order her life as completely as she possibly could, had to set little goals for herself, had to saddle herself with foolish but purposeful little disciplines. She had to budget her time, had to schedule it. She had to set small rules for herself and follow them as gospel.

She had to stop drinking.

Not because she was a textbook study in alcoholism, a person who was physically incapable of stopping after a single drink. She could have one drink and no more, but this happy fact could not camouflage the fact that she had a problem and that drinking was a part of it. Perhaps it was more symptom than cause. This didn't matter. When you have a boil under your arm, the first thing you do is drain the pus out of it; later on you can try to figure out what gave you the boil.

No more drinking, then. Not a taste, because a single drink was more than she could handle—it would throw her off her own system even if it didn't lead to another drink in due course. No more drinking, none of it, not a drop.

And it surprised her how easy it was—most of the time—to stick to the rule. There were moments when depression caught hold of her, moments when she craved a sip of wine or a stein of beer or a tangy cocktail or a belt of Scotch straight from the bottle, no ice and no glass. By and large, however, these were rare times.

With those few exceptions, all of them of relatively low intensity and fairly short duration, she found it quite easy to stay away from alcohol. Her new life was a complete departure from the old. The shift in her schedule eliminated most of the standard times when a drink was a must.

Because she did not work, the ritual of the lunch hour cocktail was easily bypassed. Because she had no friends at all, no one with whom she exchanged so much as an unnecessary word, the social aspects of drinking were completely eliminated. And, because she ate her meals in extremely inexpensive and unprepossessing restaurants where no beer or liquor was served, the before-dinner cocktail was out of the picture, as were the routines of wine or beer with the meal and a cordial after it. With no job, there was no need for a quick one when work let out at five o'clock, or another when she returned home from the office. She had no office and no work to come home from and no one to come home to, and each of these handy excuses for drinking was carefully and deliberately nudged out of her life.

But the major reason why it was not very hard to stop drinking was the momentum of the last night when she had been drinking, the night when she had touched the very bottom of the world, the night when Cherry and Evelyn had given her a guided tour of the darkest horrors of the human soul. The next morning, according to formula, she should have awakened needing a drink, a hair of the dog that had bitten her, a fast belt to take the horrid fuzzy edge off the world. This had not happened at all.

Instead she awoke with the worst hangover she had ever had in her life, a hangover of the body and the soul at once, a hangover that was a headache and a sick stomach and an inflamed conscience and a distorted time sense and a black pool of self-hatred all rolled up into one big ball of bitterness.

Instead of a craving for a drink, the very thought of alcohol in any form made her physically ill. She could not have had anything to drink that day if she had forced herself. She would have gagged on the mildest wine and would have thrown up anything she might have forced herself to swallow.

That gave her a start, a beginning. She had lived through that day without even wanting a drink, let alone having one. And by the time the immediate reaction had worn off, she had begun to develop the habit of *not* drinking just as she had previously developed the habit of drinking.

Ever since that night, she had been as unremittent a teetotaler as Carrie Nation.

Chapter 13

A day in the life of Karen Winslow:

At seven o'clock the bedside alarm clock rang. She was in the tail end of a dream just then, a nightmare of flight and pursuit, of running until her heart was bursting. She welcomed the ringing of the clock and turned it off and sat upright in bed at once, breathing deeply and steadily while her heartbeat settled itself and the last traces of the dream fled from her mind.

The dreams were getting easier now! She had ceased to mind them, had taken them as a matter of course, and as time passed they diminished in intensity. There were many nights now when she slept soundly and could not remember any dreams at all the next day.

She got out of bed, took off her nightgown and went into the bathroom. She showered, finishing with a Spartan half-minute under the cold spray. She got out of the tiny tub, toweled herself briskly dry, put on a skirt and blouse while the teakettle heated water for coffee. She made herself a cup of very strong instant coffee and sat in a chair by the window reading from the *Information Please Almanac*, the 1954 edition. She had found a copy in a second-hand bookstore for fifteen cents, 1954 having come and gone ten years ago, and she read from it every morning until eight-thirty. The book was hysterically out of date, and included tons of statistics for 1954, a year about which she was rapidly becoming the world's foremost authority. All the population figures were obsolete, as well as the economics section and the political section—for example, there seemed to be a hundred countries that had not even existed in 1954.

She read the book every morning. It was, she had decided, the best sort of mental discipline. This particular morning she read the list of Nobel Prize winners from the inception of the award to 1952. She found it interesting to notice how few of the Nobel laureates she had ever heard of. How short-lived fame was, she thought. How quickly gone.

She didn't attempt to remember what she read. That was not part of the discipline. The only important thing was to read each section very carefully, concentrating as thoroughly as possible upon the words and figures on the page before her. Concentration was the key. It mattered not at all that the names she was reading so meticulously would not stay with her ten minutes after she closed the book.

Concentration was what mattered, was one of the four steps in her program. Concentration, Meditation, Relaxation, and Recreation. Each had its place, each was neatly scheduled to fill up a part of her day.

At eight-thirty she left the hotel and went for a walk. She left Flatbush Avenue and walked through the residential side streets. She had smoked a cigarette with her morning coffee and another while she read the *Almanac*, but she did not smoke while she walked. She walked briskly and easily, her arms swinging freely at her side, breathing deeply as she went along.

It was nine-forty-five when she returned to the hotel. Some days she got back by nine-thirty; other days she walked around until ten. Her route varied considerably from day to day but each walk took the same general form. She only stopped to rest when there was something she wanted to look at—a store window, some outdoor construction, a fight, children at play. Her stops were always brief, so she spent almost the entire hour or hour and a half walking through the streets of Brooklyn.

Back at the hotel, she drew her blinds, took off all of her clothes, placed a flat cushion upon the floor and lay down on her back on the floor with her head on the pillow. She closed her eyes and worked very hard to make every muscle in her body relax. She would tighten up each group of muscles in turn then relax them as completely as she could. When she was as loose as possible, when all the muscular tension had drained away, she remained as she was, breathing very slowly and regularly, inhaling through her nostrils, exhaling through her mouth. *Today is better than yesterday,* she would tell herself. *Tomorrow will be better than today.*

It was just a modification of the old Cone routine, the Everyday-in-every-way-I'm-getting-better-and-better bit. It seemed to have a certain effect as her inner voice repeated it endlessly. And it was almost always true. Each day tended to be significantly better than the one which had preceded it.

At eleven o'clock she came out of the semi-trance state she had managed to work herself into. She took another shower—she averaged three showers a day now, and once had taken as many as six. She dressed again in the same clothes and went around the corner to a little lunch counter. She had a large glass of fresh orange juice, three eggs scrambled dry, a glass of milk, an order of whole wheat toast with butter, and two cups of black coffee. She smoked a cigarette while she drank the second cup of coffee, then left the small restaurant.

Today is *better than yesterday.*

Tomorrow will be better than today.

The library was four blocks away. It was a small branch library with the usual branch library's concentration on juvenile books. One would not choose this particular library for researching a doctoral thesis, but the collection was large enough so that she could always find something to read, and the place was properly quiet until three-thirty when the schoolchildren invaded it. She browsed through the stacks, found the book she wanted and sat down at an empty table. She began reading.

Her morning reading of the *Information Please Almanac for 1954* was discipline—cold facts, one after the other, read with meticulous concentration and no particular attention to content. Her afternoon reading was quite another matter. At the library she picked out books which interested her and read them with a purpose in mind. During the first weeks she had concentrated mostly on psychology, but since then she had wandered far afield. Novels, poetry, history, philosophy—whatever seemed suitable to her mood and to the state of her mind. This day she was reading the collected poems of Wallace Stevens. She did not understand much of what she was reading. Many of the allusions were difficult to grasp and many of the images did not entirely register. But she stayed with the book for three hours and a good deal did soak in.

She returned the volume to its place in the stacks, left the library, lit a cigarette, walked through the neighborhood with no particular purpose in mind.

She had come along nicely with her meditation. There were

many things she understood now about herself and her world that she had not begun to recognize before.

She had thought, for example, that she had adjusted readily and completely to her life with Rae Cooper. She realized now how completely wrong she had been. If that life had been so suitable, if she had adjusted to it so perfectly she would never have started drinking heavily. The one was a definite result of the other.

And she could pretty well see how it had come about. The trauma of pregnancy and Ronnie's betrayal culminating in attempted suicide. The combination of deep insecurity and loneliness and a fear of the male sex had made her a good candidate for homosexuality. The initial shock of Rae's embrace had scared her. Then, when she had decided to accept Rae's love—and this had been as much an intellectual decision as an emotional one, she had realized one day with a flash of insight—when this had happened, she had thrown herself into Rae's world with a vengeance. All the doubts and hesitations were shoved violently into the background, pushed out of sight and ostensibly out of mind. All of the conflicts were packed away in a closet or swept under a rug, and she had thought that they were gone, and she had been as wrong as one could be.

Because inside her private self she was the same lost Karen. That was why a part of her consciousness so often sat in the corner; observing but uninvolved, watching but untouched. That was why she had developed such a taste for alcohol in any of its myriad forms. Reality kept threatening to intrude upon the little world she had constructed for herself, and it was imperative that she keep those hard facts in the background—shut in the closet or tucked under the carpet.

Every day a little more of the past was brought into the light of day and examined closely and clearly. Each day she saw herself with a little more perspective and a little less confusion. And each day she could ask herself the same questions with a little more hope of hitting on the right answer.

What would she do next? One thing that she was beginning to see was that she could not run away again, that she would have to run back—back to Manhattan, back to Leon Gordon's office, back to her job. This would be harder than building an entirely new life, but she could see that it was also quite essential. It was too easy to fall into a constant pattern of escape, and she could not afford to do this. She had an awful tendency to run away from situations. It was necessary to face them directly and deal with them on their own terms.

The job had an importance, too. Before it had been a static situation, pleasant and easy but with no future. It was time she began looking at things in terms of the future. A job that meant nothing but the investment of forty hours a week in return for a comfortable salary was stagnant and meaningless. A job ought to point somewhere, ought to lead to something.

Gordon liked and respected her. She could be more than a pretty telephone voice for him. She could perform more important services and learn his business more thoroughly. Women could become successful show business agents. Not many of them did, but it was possible, and she seemed to have as good a background for the profession as anyone. If she expressed an interest, if she worked at it, he would let her learn the game. He might even let herself work her way up in his office, so that she could handle tasks of increasing responsibility. And he wasn't young. Sooner or later he would want to retire, or at least drift into semi-retirement. If she handled things properly, she could wind up in a very good position.

This meant a complete re-orientation on her part. Her job could not be the simple convenience it had been, the dues you paid in return for enough money to live decently. She would have to care about it and take an interest in it and work harder at it.

She also had to find the right direction for her love life. At first she had thought she would have to push sex out of the picture, perhaps forever. This was possible, she knew; people did it all the time, sublimating, forcing all their energies in another direction until they literally forgot about sex. But she came to see that this was not an entirely satisfactory solution, although it remained a possibility.

Perhaps, she thought, she could be happy with men. One bad experience didn't mean all that much. One bout of drinking had not made her an irredeemable alcoholic, and one bout of lesbianism certainly did not make her inevitably homosexual.

Perhaps she could go back to Rae. It was possible that she could only be happy with another woman. There were elements of her relationships with Ronnie that suggested she had been basically homosexual from the start, and it was certainly possible that she was incapable of finding any real happiness with a man. If she could overcome the guilt she had felt with Rae, if she could make a real adjustment and get everything out in the open, then perhaps things could work out for them.

So many things to decide . . .

She had a simple dinner at a cafeteria at six-thirty and read a newspaper while she drank her coffee. There was a chamber music concert at the Brooklyn Museum of Science at eight-thirty. She returned to the hotel, showered, changed her clothes, and walked to the museum. It was a long walk but the night was cool and she didn't mind the distance. The music held her attention completely. This, she knew, was a direct result of her new living pattern. Before she had always found her attention wandering at concerts. Even when she enjoyed them she would have long periods of inattentiveness when her mind would let go of the music entirely and wander off along paths of its own. Now, however, concentration had become a habit; when she went to a concert, which she did two or three times a week, she was caught up in the music entirely.

It was almost eleven when she left the concert and she did not want to walk back to the hotel at that hour. She hailed a taxi and rode back to the hotel. She did not take cabs often, but she could afford one now and then. Her meals had cost her $2.15, her hotel room worked out to a dollar and a half a day, and the concert had been free. With the dollar for the taxi, her total expenditures for the day were under five dollars. At that rate she could live on unemployment insurance and wind up saving money.

In her room she undressed, took the fourth and final shower of the day, set her alarm clock and got into bed. She wondered whether the shower habit would last when she got back to an ordinary living pattern. It might be inconvenient, she thought, running home from the office every few hours to hop into the tub.

She stretched out in bed and went through the routine of relaxing each group of muscles in turn, then let her mind go gradually blank. The first week she had taken a single sleeping pill each night, and this had helped. Since then, however, she had had no trouble sleeping without any assistance from pills. Now she closed her eyes and fell asleep easily.

Today is better than yesterday.

Tomorrow will be better than today.

A day in the life of Karen Winslow.

Chapter 14

It was Tuesday, and it was raining. After she had showered and had coffee and read from the almanac, she realized, suddenly, that it was time. She took her usual walk, knowing he would not be at the office yet, and when she returned she called him from the telephone in her room. It was the first time she used the telephone since she first moved into the Rainier Arms.

His answering service took the call, which pleased her—he evidently had not hired another girl to take her place. She left her name and number with the answering service, and he returned the call within five minutes.

"Karen, honey," the agent said. "I wanted to call you a hundred times but you never gave me your number. You all right?"

"Yes," she said. "Yes, I am." It was so strange to be talking with someone, she thought. So odd. She had not talked with anyone whom she really knew for such a long time.

"Everything working out?"

"Yes. Perfectly."

"That's good news. When are you coming back?"

"Is the job still open?"

"It's always been yours," he said. "Whenever you're ready."

"Monday?"

"Sure thing."

She needed a cigarette. "Hold on a second," she said, and lit one. Funny, she thought, how one needed little conversational props like that. She knew that she would be smoking more heavily from now on. Before she moved to the Rainier Arms she had been chain-smoking constantly, working her way through close to three packs a day. The last few days she had been down to four or five cigarettes a day—one with morning coffee, one after each meal, and one or two more at various times. Before long she would be up to a pack a day, but she knew too that she would never smoke as heavily as she had done before. She would not need to.

She said, "There's one favor I'd like to ask. Could you possibly let me have Adrian March's phone number?"

"March?"

"That's right."

"You won't get him now, he's hardly ever home. You can leave a number with his answering service if you want."

"That's what I'll do, then."

He gave her the number, and she wrote it down. "Thank you," she said. "And I'll be in Monday morning, if you're sure you still want me."

"Don't worry on that score. Monday, kid."

She put the phone down, finished her cigarette, walked to the window. A cold gray drizzling day. She had not minded the rain while she had been walking that morning; somehow the day seemed so right to her that the weather could not spoil it. She turned from the window, went to the phone again and dialed the number Gordon had given her. She left her own name and number with Adrian March's answering service and sat down patiently to wait for his call.

⁓•⁓

"Karen? Is it really you?"

"Yes," she said. "Hello."

"Well, I thought I'd lost you forever. What on earth happened to you? You quit Gordon, I gather."

"I took a vacation," she said. "A long one. I'll be going back to work Monday."

"He was telling the truth, then? An extraordinary thing for an agent to do! I knew he was at least bright enough not to discharge you, so I assumed you'd quit. Where *are* you?"

"In Brooklyn."

"No one is *ever* in Brooklyn. Not even the Dodgers are in Brooklyn, dear girl. May I see you?"

"That's why I called."

"I'd offer to come for you . . ."

"No, I thought I'd meet you in Manhattan."

"That's infinitely better, as I'm sure I'd get lost in Brooklyn. I understand everyone does. Everyone who goes there at any rate. Where shall we meet?"

"Your apartment?"

"If you'd like. Do you know how to get there?"

"No."

He gave her the address. "I'm downtown now," he said, "and I've got a few places to stop before I head home. Shall we meet in about two hours?"

"That's fine," she said.

～ᘔᗏᑕ～

He had a three-room apartment on East 83rd Street near the river, beautifully furnished with a lovely view. "All of this comes courtesy of the soap manufacturers," he said, with a grand wave of his hand. "The true road to a life of happiness and luxury is paved with the diligent prostitution of one's God-given talent. If this nation were a monarchy I trust it would have a harlot for its queen. Can I get you a drink, Karen?"

"Coffee or a soft drink," she said.

"Ah! The water wagon?"

"I'm afraid so."

"So that's where you disappeared to? Extraordinary." He started toward the liquor cabinet, then drew up abruptly. "I hope you're not one of those dreary reformed alcoholics who cringes in the presence of liquor? Or foams at the mouth?"

She laughed. "Drink yourself into a coma if you like," she said. "I'm not the evangelistic type, I'm afraid. And it won't make me break out in a rash, either. I'm a properly disciplined little girl."

He made himself a generous drink, then brought her a ginger ale from the kitchen. They sat together on the couch and touched glasses.

"You must tell all," he said. "The Remarkable Saga of Karen Winslow, or, Can a Poor but Honest Girl from the Big City Find Happiness in the Wilds of Brooklyn?"

"Words by Horatio Alger," she said. "Music by Sigmund Romberg."

"Precisely."

She gave him the censored version of the past weeks, omitting only the sexual side of the entire affair. She told him she had been drinking more and enjoying it less and let it seem as though her drinking alone had sent her on her pilgrimage to Flatbush. He seemed very interested in the precise methods she had used for her little project of self-rehabilitation. The *Information Please Almanac for 1954* was a special source of joy to him.

"Remarkable," he said. "What was the population of Racine, Wis., in 1950? Do you recall?"

"I don't remember any of it," she said. "Just an occasional fact here and there."

"For example?"

"Elbridge Gerry was the only Vice-President of the United States to be buried in Washington."

"Honestly?"

"Honestly."

He refilled his glass. "Why on earth do you happen to remember that?" he asked.

"I'm damned if I know."

He started to laugh and she laughed with him, and it was the first time she had laughed in far too long. The first time she'd talked to anyone, the first time she'd laughed, the first time for so very many things.

He said, "Dinner?"

"Oh, if you have plans . . ."

"None at all. That regimen of yours sounds frightening, especially in respect to food. I can't believe your diet for the past little while would make a gourmet jealous, do you suppose?"

"Probably not."

He thought for a moment. "Ordinarily I'd suggest Voisin," he said, "but if you've been leading the simple life a proper French repast would probably make you ill. How does a very thick, very fine steak sound? With a baked potato and salad with Roquefort and very strong coffee and—"

"Sold," she said.

The whole scheme was not an easy one. He was simply not a lecherous old man, and he was very much a friend and just as much a gentleman. All through the evening, from dinner onward, she tried to make herself as obvious as possible without being unforgivably cheap in the process. She could not believe that he was too dense to realize what it was that she wanted, and yet he would not take up the hint.

They were at his apartment now, once more. Dinner, a Broadway show—how he had gotten good tickets so late she could not imagine—and they were once more in his living room, she with another glass of ginger ale, he with a snifter of very old Armagnac. It astonished her how very much he could drink without one noticing it. He never seemed to be drinking a great deal, and yet he was constantly drinking one thing or another. None of it showed; he was exactly the same in manner and appearance no matter how much he drank.

This in itself had been a good test for her. She'd been fairly certain that she would not want a drink even if she was with someone who was drinking, but it was a hypothesis that had to be tested, and she had been at least a little bit worried. But she had turned out to have not the slightest desire for a drink. He had sherry before dinner and burgundy with it and brandy after, and she had only coffee without ever feeling the desire for anything stronger.

Now, if he would only cooperate . . .

It had seemed such a simple matter when she first thought of it. He was a man, and one whom she liked and trusted. And she was a woman, and she knew he liked her and guessed that he probably found her attractive. All she had to do was give him an opening, make it mildly obvious that she wouldn't mind if he made a pass at her. When he did, she would let things progress from that point of their own accord.

How else would she be able to find out what was right for her? She could not pick up some man off the street—she would hate that and rightly so, whether she was homosexual or not. But with someone she knew, someone she liked, it might be different.

And either way she would be able to find out once and for all. She could find out whether she had gone to Rae only because of what had happened with Ronnie or if she had been basically gay from the deep beginnings. Either way, she would find out.

She stood up, walked glass in hand to the window. She heard him get to his feet and move to join her. When he was at her side, she half-turned to him.

"The view is lovely," she said. "You can see for miles."

"It's best in the morning. With the sun just edging up over the East River and the reflection on the water."

She didn't say anything, but turned to face him and tilted her face upward toward him. Her eyes were partly lidded now, her lips slightly open. She felt very theatrical and waited for him to take up the cue.

Maddeningly, he said, "So you want to be more than Leon's decorative receptionist? You want to learn the business?"

"You think it's a bad idea?"

"No, not at all. Although you don't seem entirely the type. You're more the innocent flower than the serpent under it, aren't you?"

"Perhaps."

"And not the bold and brassy type at all."

She didn't say anything.

"It's rather late," he said, "Shall I see you home?"

"All the way to Brooklyn?"

"Why . . ."

"If I don't stay here," she said, "how am I going to see the sunrise on the river?"

For a moment he looked as though someone had dropped a weight upon him from a great height. He backed off, then stepped closer to her. "Heavens," he said.

She did not say anything.

"Karen," he said, and took her in his arms. She pressed against him and he kissed her, held her close. She did not know how she felt, was not able to tell. "Karen," he said again, and kissed her again, and his arms were tight around her. His mouth tasted of brandy and cigarettes.

There was one problem with the disciplines she had practiced, the continent life she had led—she had lived so long without being kissed or touched, had schooled herself so carefully to avoid even thinking in those terms, that everything was rather odd and unfamiliar to her. But she let herself ease into the role, returned with him to the couch, sat with him, kissed him and was kissed by him, and sat still in his arms while he opened her clothing and held her young body in his hands.

There were no words except when he repeated her name, gently, and tenderly. She was afraid to speak, and she was glad that he said nothing but her name, breathing it into her hair, her throat, her breasts, as he touched her and kissed her and made love to her.

She felt nothing, but this did not surprise her. She had anticipated as much. Response, excitement, enjoyment—these things might come later if they were to come at all. But if she could endure his embrace, if she at least found nothing offensive in making love with a man, then perhaps in the future all of this would transform into excitement and passion.

She had been certain he would be a good lover. He was a much older man, and that was good on two counts. The rough, hurried embrace of a younger man would have frightened her. Besides that, she knew that he was a lover of great experience. He was sensitive and aware, and if any man would be likely to make her find delight in his embrace, Adrian would be the man.

He kissed her face, her throat, her breasts. She had to fight with herself to keep from tensing up as he removed her clothing. It seemed an invasion of privacy, seemed as though she were being exposed more than she wanted to be. But the tricks of relaxation helped her now. She forced her muscles to stay limp and at ease, forced her whole body to remain passive, placid.

His lips played at her breasts, and she put one hand upon the back of his head and cradled his head against her breasts. Why did she feel so observed? Why did it seem as though she were on a stage, with the eyes of the world upon her? Perhaps because in a sense she *was* playing a role, she told herself. Perhaps because she was acting, because she was pretending to be moved by passion when the true motive force was—what? Curiosity? Not precisely that, perhaps, but something very much akin to it.

"Karen," he murmured, and she felt his hand on her knee, petting, so gently.

She was gritting her teeth. She forced herself to stop, and his hand moved up underneath her dress, up onto the very soft skin of her thighs. He touched her very lightly, and his touch tickled her in an unpleasant sort of way. As though her skin were crawling, she thought. She closed her eyes and breathed very deeply, fighting the slight quiver of revulsion that passed over her.

He mistook the quick intake of breath for a show of passion, and he breathed her name again and kissed her lips and let his hand move higher beneath her dress. She fought her own feelings and threw her arms taut around him, kissed him, passed her tongue into his brandy-and-tobacco mouth. She concentrated on kissing him and pressing his body against her breasts and tried not to be aware of his hand.

Just go through it, she told herself. Just let it happen, just let it hurry up and happen . . .

Would they do it on the couch? Would she lift her dress and drop her pants, and would they do it right there? Or would they go into the bedroom? That might be impossibly awkward, she thought. Getting up and breaking the mood and walking into the bedroom and getting undressed and all. How did one manage it? Just race for the bed like maniacs?

When his fingers touched her, found her, there was an involuntary muscle spasm, a sudden unpredictable knotting of the muscles there. It was acutely painful, and she bore down on every muscle, all in an effort to work the kink out of the muscle. She let go, then, and the spasm relaxed. His fingers went on touching her, touching her, and she stayed very calm, calm, cool . . .

If only her *mind* would relax. She had mastered her body, her muscles were no longer tense, but she could not blank out her crazy damned brain and it was driving her to distraction. Stop thinking, she told herself. Just relax, just go blank . . .

His lips brushed her ear, nibbled at the fleshy lobe. "I'll meet you in the bedroom," he whispered very softly "Through that door . . ."

She went into the bedroom. Of course, she thought, that was the simplest way. No mad fumble on the couch, no mad scramble hand-in-hand to the bed. She closed the door and got quickly out of her clothes in the darkness. Then she drew down the bed clothing and lay down on the sheet, waiting for him.

She waited, and the door opened, and she strained to see him in the darkness. He was naked too, she knew. And moving toward her, joining her on the bed.

"Karen," he said, "my little darling."

They kissed, and she felt their bare bodies press together. He had hair on his chest and she felt it against her breasts. Ronnie didn't have hair on his chest, she thought. Neither did Rae, she thought idiotically, and she almost laughed. He kissed her again and pushed her shoulders so that she lay back on her bed and he hovered over her, running his hands over every part of her body like a blind man reading a book written in Braille.

Oh, please, please, let it work out . . .

Then he was touching her legs, then kissing them, and she guessed what he was going to do. A sigh escaped her lips, and then he kissed her.

Wings clouds and ribbons of silk. Birds, flowers and wisps of straw across the dimpled face of the moon. A stream flowing down the side of a silver mountain.

Yes, yes, oh yes.

A hot afternoon laced with breezes. Sun and sand and a rising tide. Orchids lilies rainbow. Blue and gold fishes at the black bottom of the sea.

Yes, yes. More, more . . .

Geese flying south. A hole in the earth and the sea running dry. A train on a bridge. Five hundred trumpets and one violin. Spiders a bee a hummingbird.

No don't stop. No no don't stop please don't stop . . .

But he had stopped, and he was moving on the bed, and her mind froze in time. A soldier, grinning, rushing for her with fixed bayonet . . .

Towers and swords and knives. Guns poles battering rams clubs razors blood death hell!

When he touched her she screamed. His flesh on her flesh and she screamed, shrieked, shrill, loud, and rolling away and crying out into the night and pushing him off and shouting out no no no no . . .

"NO! Please, NO!"

Chapter 15

She was kneeling in a corner of the living room with her head in her hands. She could barely remember running there from the bedroom. She was on her knees; her elbows were pressed against her thighs, her face buried in her hands, and she was doing everything she could to keep from falling apart at the seams. Her eyes were welled up with tears but she had not cried yet. The tendons in her throat were tighter than bow strings. She wished desperately that she were somewhere else. Anywhere else.

"Karen—"

She could not bring herself to face him. How could she have done this to him? To begin by trying so desperately to use him, and then to cheat him out of what she had promised, recoiling and fleeing from him like a damned idiot virgin.

Why?

"I brought you a robe, Karen, Karen, don't hate me, dear. I'm sorry for what happened. Karen—"

She spun around, "*You're* sorry? Don't . . . don't be ridiculous! I'm the one who's sorry. I didn't mean . . . I didn't know . . . oh, I can't even talk straight!"

He made her take the robe. She struggled to her feet and got it around her shoulders. He was wearing a plaid robe and a pair of bedroom slippers, and he was holding a drink in his hand. For a moment she came very close to asking for a drink herself.

"I did the worst thing I've ever done in my life," she said.

"Oh, don't be ridiculous."

"You must hate me."

"Hate you?"

She turned away. "You should have gone ahead and raped me. Or slapped my idiot head off."

"For what? For depriving me of something I had no particular claim on in the first place? Nonsense."

She found her pack of cigarettes and lit one. Without looking at him she said, "Do you know what I did, Adrian? I called you earlier because I wanted you to make love to me. I planned everything. The entire thing, I planned it all."

"That's not all that unusual."

"No, you don't understand! I didn't do it because I *wanted* it, because I *desired* you. I did it to find something out."

He didn't say anything. She turned toward him. "I owe you a full explanation. Let's sit down."

"You don't owe me anything, Karen."

"Oh, but I do."

"Not really. If you want to get dressed and go home, then that's precisely what you should do."

"No, I want to talk."

"You're sure of that?"

"I *have* to talk. If I could just unwind for a moment first. Would it be all right if I got under the shower for a few minutes?"

He smiled. "Cold showers only work for boy scouts, dear. Yes, of course you may use the shower. I'll wait for you."

She scooped up her clothes from the bedroom and hurried into the bathroom and got under the shower. The significance of the shower was not lost on her, and she knew it must be clear to him as well. She was taking a shower now for the same reason that she had taken endless showers at the Rainier Arms. To cleanse herself—because she felt so very unclean.

You found out, she told herself. You acted like an idiot, you lost yourself in yourself and forgot that there were other people in the world.

She had been all right when it was just acting, going through the motions and enduring caresses and feigning passion. But near the end her passion had not been artificial. Near the end, when he gave her the kiss that Rae had bestowed so often, when he bestowed the caress that one woman would bestow upon another, her passion had been perfectly genuine.

And when he stopped playing the woman and moved to play the man, her defenses were down. She had lost control of the game, she could not play-act any more. Her reaction had to be a real one, a true one. And now she knew what she was and what she was not.

But what a dreadful, dishonest, inhuman way to find out!

He was waiting in the living room for her. He had made a cup of coffee, and she sat down gratefully with it and sipped it. She felt a little better now. Calmer, once more in control.

"I have to tell you things," she said. "Adrian, do you remember when I told you a boyfriend of mine had walked out on me or something? I don't remember the details . . ."

"Yes, I remember."

"All right. It wasn't a boyfriend, it was a girlfriend. The girl I had been living with for some time. I'm a lesbian, Adrian. Or at least I was then. And oh, let me start at the beginning, it'll be easier that way."

This time she told him everything. She didn't gush like a fool because she was calm enough to exert a little control over the flow of her words. But she started with Ronnie and included everything important right up to the present. She told him things that no one else knew and he listened without an interruption.

"So now you know it all," she said finally. "From a mistress to an attempted suicide to a lesbian to a drunk to a pervert to a recluse to what I was tonight. I never meant it to come out this way, Adrian. I swear I never thought it could be like this, the way I reacted. I thought that I would just . . . just let you make love to me, and if it was unbearable I would simply endure it, and if it was good so much the better, and . . . oh, it sounds harebrained now, doesn't it? I thought that if nothing else I would at least find out about myself one way or another. What I was, what I wanted, all of that."

"And?"

She looked at him.

"Well?" he said. "Didn't you find out?"

"I don't understand, All I did was do something horrible to you and make a fool of myself and—"

"Listen to me for a moment." He looked down into his drink, then looked up at her again. "You went through a fairly intense period of auto-analysis, Karen. I can't believe that you failed to realize one thing—that you're most apt to feel guilty because you *want* to feel guilty."

"I know that."

"All right. It applies tonight, too. There's no earthly reason why you should blame yourself on my account. Whatever for? Do you think the fact that I've been denied a thrill is going to give me either a bruised ego or cancer of the prostate? It won't. I will live through it. I *have* lived through it."

"But—"

"Wait a moment. And if you think that it will lessen my opinion of you, that I will either hate or despise you, you're also mistaken. No such thing, Karen. I find you at least as admirable as before, if not more so."

He finished his drink, set the glass down on the coffee table. "Let me continue," he said. "You've said that tonight was essentially a scientific experiment, correct? You can take it further than that. It was a successful experiment. It gave you an answer—not, perhaps, the answer you may have hoped for, but the answer you needed to have. Item: you found lovemaking with a man endurable but unpleasant, endurable so long as you kept your emotional guard up, as long as you held yourself in careful control. Item: you found lovemaking suddenly exciting in a situation where consciously or unconsciously you were able to react as though it was a woman who was making love to you. Item: in this state, with the control removed and the reins out of your hands, the sudden shocking prospect of sexual relations with a man drew an honest, basic, unconscious and wholly legitimate reaction—you rejected it entirely. Conclusion—"

"I'm a lesbian," she broke in.

"So it would seem. You could have gone to a psychoanalyst for five years before you got so revealing a catharsis. Five days a week at twenty-five dollars a visit—do you realize you've just saved yourself sixty-five hundred dollars?"

She managed to smile.

"So you're a lesbian," he went on. "You were prepared to accept that possibility before, weren't you? Is it harder to accept it now?"

"No, I guess not."

"It's not horrible, you know. In the theater it's not even unusual enough to be considered interesting. If you were a minister's daughter in Horse Dropping, Montana, then you'd have a problem. If you had a conventional sense of sin you'd be caught up in something of a conflict. But you strike me as a generally pragmatic person whose moral principles are more or less limited to the Golden Rule. It may bother you to hear this, Karen, but I don't think you've got much of a problem any more. I think you've solved it, and done so very well."

She took a sip of coffee, set the cup down in her saucer, took a cigarette and let him light it for her. She sat for several moments in silence, smoking the cigarette, finishing the coffee.

Finally she said, "You're right, Adrian. Everything you said. I should have seen that myself, shouldn't I?"

"You would have, sooner or later. You were in a state of shock."

"Yes, and I probably still am. Adrian, what should I do now?"

"Get some sleep."

"I mean—"

"I know what you mean. What should you do as far as the girl is concerned? Rachel—is that what you said her name was?"

"Yes."

"What do you think you should do?"

"I don't even know what I think tonight."

"Well," he said. "First of all, it's not a decision you have to make tonight. But I think you should probably go to her, if only to find out how you feel and what you really want. If nothing else, you must realize now that people don't exist in a vacuum and that decisions can never be made in a vacuum. Do you love her?"

"I don't know. But . . ."

"But what?"

"It's a place to start, isn't it?"

"That's right"

"And if it works, fine, and if it doesn't—"

"Then it doesn't, Karen. And no harm done to anyone."

"And they all lived happily ever after," she said slowly.

"Exactly. And in the meantime, because it is very late and you would not want to make an old man worry about you, you will go into the bedroom where our little drama unfolded and you will go to sleep while I have another drink or two prefatory to stretching out on the couch. And no arguments, no you-take-the-bed-and-leave-me-the-couch please, if you don't mind. Just humor me. Unless you would be nervous sleeping under the same roof with a man."

"Oh, don't be silly."

"Then the bedroom's yours. You'll like it better this time. You were a bit confused and disturbed before."

"I probably still am, but at least my mind's working a little better now. Everything's worked out right, hasn't it? But I'll always be sorry for using you that way. No matter how you say it doesn't matter, I'll always feel a little badly about it."

His eyes probed hers. "Really?"

"Yes."

"Because you used me," he said, as if quoting. "Such a silly term.

Everyone uses everyone—that's what interpersonal relationships are, nothing but a grandified term for mutual exploitation. But let me explain something for you. You hurt me—how? With a few minutes of sexual frustration? I've been over that since a couple of moments after you scurried out of the bedroom. Completely over it.

"But I'll tell you something. I may never get over feeling so enormously flattered that you cast me as the guinea pig in your small experiment. That out of the entire world you very scientifically singled me out as the man with whom you would investigate love. Hurt me? Karen, dear Karen, you've given me a glow that will never entirely wear off."

"I don't understand . . ."

"Of course you don't," he said "You couldn't possibly understand. But someday you may. In thirty years, or forty, you may."

Chapter 16

He was up and out of the apartment before she awoke. It took her a few moments to orient herself. Then she showered quickly, made herself a cup of coffee, and left his apartment. It amused her to notice how incomplete it felt to go out without having read the *Information Please Almanac for 1954.* As though she'd gone out without putting on her shoes.

She rode a bus downtown to Twenty-Third Street and Second Avenue, then hesitated on the corner for a few moments, waiting, preparing herself. When she was as ready as she felt likely to be she walked to Rae's apartment, to the apartment they had shared.

And if she doesn't want me? And if we try and nothing happens for us? And if . . .

Bridges. To be crossed when she reached them, and not before.

She hesitated again in front of the building. It was still early enough so that Rae might be asleep, she thought Rae had always liked to sleep late. Maybe . . .

No. No stalling.

She marched bravely up the steps and into the hallway and rang the proper bell and waited, waited. There was an answering buzz to open the inner vestibule door, and she opened the door while the buzzer sounded and walked quickly to Rae's door. *Their* door. The apartment's door, at any rate.

And knocked on the door.

The girl who opened the door was not Rae at all. She was short and dark and slender, with very large eyes made larger still by an abundance of dark eye-shadow. Then Rae had moved, she thought. Now how on earth could she find her? And how did she get out of the lease?

"Can I help you?"

"No, I'm sorry," she said, recovering. "I've made a mistake. I was looking for the girl who used to live here, I didn't know she'd moved."

"You mean Rae? She had a morning meeting with an editor." She started. "You're not Karen, are you?"

"Yes, I am."

"Rae talked about you. I . . . uh . . . my name is Lois. Karen and I . . . say, would you like to come in for a cup of coffee? I mean I don't want to keep you standing out in the hall like a Fuller Brush Man."

"No, thank you, but don't bother."

"No bother, really. You sure?"

"No, I don't have the time," she said.

"I see." Lois shifted her weight from one foot to the other. She said, "Uh . . . Rae and I are . . . uh . . . together now. I don't know just how things wound up between you two or anything, but—"

"We're just old friends," Karen said.

"Sure, but the thing is—"

"I just dropped in to say goodbye," she went on. "I'm going to the Coast. San Francisco. And I didn't want to call, you know, because we'd been so long without seeing each other, and the way we broke off. Well. You understand."

"Of course." The girl seemed relieved—a possible complication had turned out to be nothing of the sort. "Listen, you're not going to run off, are you? Because Rae ought to be home in an hour or so, and she'll be sorry she missed you."

"I wish I could stay, but my flight's leaving in an hour and a half and it takes almost an hour to get to the airport. I left all my things at the East Side Terminal and now I have to cab over there and get there in time to make the limousine connections. You'll tell her I came over?"

"Oh, of course."

"Good." She smiled. "I'm sure you're happy together?"

"Very," Lois said.

"I'm glad to hear that."

How nicely you carried that off, she told herself, turning the corner and heading north on Third Avenue. How very nicely you managed that. How poised you're becoming, how glibly you handle yourself. Flying to San Francisco, limousine connections, just dropped in to say goodbye—how very Bette Davis.

Unless it's painful, my sweet.

The line sounded in her mind, the private cliché, and she remembered what they had been to each other and what they had shared, the laughter, the love, the good times, all of it.

It would have been easy enough to dramatize, to pause in a

doorway and wipe tears from her eyes, to smile bravely, to choke back a sob. She was unable to do it, however.

Because it was no time for sorrow, no time for tears. She felt no sorrow, not now. No pain, no loss, no sorrow. She had not been hurt, she had lost nothing.

What had she told Adrian last night? That Rae might be a place to start. No more than that. If there was something for them to take up together, all well and good, and they could try the shoe and see if it pinched or not. And if there was nothing, so be it.

She was in no desperate need of anyone. Before, after she left the hospital, loneliness had been painful; now it was not. Before, after all of that hurt and in the midst of all that confusion, she had been starved for love; now she was not. If love came along, fine. If she had to wait awhile, also fine.

No sorrow. No tears.

And, until the right thing came at its own pace, she had as much as she needed. Her room at the Rainier Arms had been comfortable all along; it would be as comfortable now. Brooklyn had been an ideal place to live; it would be just as ideal now, and the slight inconvenience of a subway ride each morning and night would not be such a dreadful cross to bear. She still had her hotplate and teakettle for morning coffee. She still had her copy of the *Information Please Almanac for 1954*. She would be working days—and working hard, learning, advancing—but she would still have her nights for the library and concerts, and she would still have the weekends for long walks and visits to empty churches.

It's worked out, she thought. It's worked out right.

She looked at her watch. It was almost eleven, and there was no need to wait any longer, no need at all. She stepped to the curb, hailed a cab, gave the driver Leon Gordon's address. She had told him she would start Monday morning, and it was just Wednesday now; he would be surprised to see her.

She lit a cigarette. No tears, she thought, none at all. And she blew out smoke and let her face relax in a smile. She had had enough of sorrow, she thought. She was all better now. She was alive.

EXCERPT: *THIRTY*

January 7

How confusing!

The trouble with a diary is that you have to decide who you are writing it to. (I mean to whom you are writing it. No, I don't. I mean what I said. If this is going to work at all, I'd be well advised to write as I talk. Which is not a matter of dese and dem and dose, because I am after all a literate and wordsworthy person, acknowledged to be fairly bright for a lady. But there is no point, in these pages, being a nut about grammatical perfection. Or sitting around hung up over the spelling of a word.)

Interesting, though, that the Personal Diary of Jan Giddings Kurland should begin *How confusing*. Interesting. Curiouser and Curiouser . . .

My lawyers. Curiouser and Curiouser, Attorneys-at-Law.

Confusing because I've been spending the morning and much of the afternoon pacing around trying to figure out how to start this. What tone to take. Whether to begin each entry "Dear Diary" as girls do in books—and thus probably in real life as well, life imitating bad art as it does. Or whether to write each day's entry as if to Howie, if for no better reason than that the sneak will probably read this sooner or later anyway, and that if each entry began "Dear Howie" he could do so with a somewhat clearer conscience, assuming, that is, that conscience is still a valid concept while discussing Howie, that his has not atrophied from lack of use, like a nun's cunt.

Howie is Howard Kurland, my husband. I am Janet Kurland, the former Janet Giddings. Howie is thirty-two. He is tall, he has brown hair, his eyes are also brown, he—

No, impossible. I cannot get hung up on things like that or this book will never get anywhere.

It's probably too late anyway. The year is already a week old. The night before last was Twelfth Night. We put the Christmas tree out for the garbage. As it was, we had waited a little too long, but I'm a traditionalist. Every year when Twelfth Night comes we take out the mangy old Christmas tree, and I open my birthday presents! Christmas is officially over and I'm officially a year older.

When I was a girl (I don't like that sentence, I mean phrase, I don't like that phrase, not at all, the ring of it, the echo of an old woman's voice speaking those words, I am still a girl, I want still to be a girl, twenty-nine is not that old, twenty-nine too old, twenty-nine years, my thirtieth year, God!). When I was younger (cheat!) it balanced off, Twelfth Night and birthday, because the end of Christmas was sorrowful, in a way, but the happiness of a birthday made up for it. Well, it still balances, but the other way around. I was glad to get that broken-down tree out of the house, glad to see Christmas over for a year, no more decorations all over the neighborhood, no more of the forced hilarity of the holiday season.

Being twenty-nine, having embarked on one's thirtieth year, on the other hand, was the greatest drag imaginable.

So. I don't keep diaries. I'm not good at it, I start off all ambitious (like everything else) and by the end of January I don't want to be bothered with the job of recording each day's trivia, and sometime in mid-February I remember that the diary, poor thing, poor orphan, is stuck up on some closet shelf, and I find it and destroy it unread, as if the future would be poisoned by the simple existence of the past, let alone its tangible presence.

(I don't know what that last means. But I will not cross anything out. That's part of what this diary is all about.)

And so to put down, now, once and forever what this diary *is* all about. Not a place to record everything that happens, not a source of guilt when a few days go by without an entry. But merely a place to write messages to the girl in the mirror.

I found myself, all afternoon, coming face to face with my reflections. Not my verbal reflections but with mirror images. Literally. The mirror over the bathroom sink, on the bedroom closet door, the car's rear-view mirror, all sorts of mirrors. And I kept studying myself either critically or generously, and also I found myself just staring blankly into my own baby browns, *staring unseeing* is I guess the phrase, while I tried to puzzle out how this diary business ought to be aimed. And then I decided to write it to the girl in the mirror.

Which is to say not to my own self, because the girl in the mirror lives in her own world, really. That world must be rather like this one, because the girl's life puts the same lines in her poor face that Reality (I saw a hippie button that says "Reality is a Crutch.") has been putting with increasing frequency in mine. So I write to you, Mirror Jan. To a nonexistent person who exists as another self or I. Thus I need only tell you the things I find interesting. I don't have to describe myself all that much, do I? You and I must look at each other half a hundred times a day. And I don't have to apologize for the occasional run-on sentence, or for other errors of style which would be inexcusable if this were pretending to be some sort of Capotean nonfiction novel.

For that matter, I trust you won't mind if I cease herewith to address you in the second person—it does seem rather precious. And that you won't be dismayed if days or even weeks pass without word from me. Because it seems to me that the reason I generally abandon diaries is that they turn into chores, and my track record with chores of any description is Not Good.

And, actually, I rather would like this to turn out well. I don't know exactly what I hope to accomplish, but—

But bullshit. I know what this is supposed to accomplish. It is supposed to be therapy. It is supposed to keep the everyday house-wife from going quietly or unquietly over the edge. From dropping out of her tree. From wigging out.

Why do we have so many euphemisms for unpleasant truths? So many cute ways to describe ourselves if, for example, we are drunk. Or if we go insane.

I am not going insane.

I am going insane.

I am sick of this, for now. I think.

January 8

Last night was horrible.

Howard came home with what I think the lower orders would describe as a hair up his ass. Just a wee bit too much aggravation at the office and just a wee bit more booze than he positively needed in the club car. When I picked him up at the train he started bitching at me for not having had air put in the front left tire. It is not flat, but then neither is it round, and we had decided that I would have them put air in the tire, a service they perform willingly when they sell you gas. Had I failed to get gas? No. Then I meant to say that I had gone into the gas station without getting the tire filled? Right, guilty. Well, what the hell was the matter with me, anyway? A good question, and one which, although I said nothing, was not entirely original on his part; I had been asking myself much the same thing all day.

He had a couple more drinks with dinner. I don't exactly blame him. Dinner, let's be honest, stank. A noble experiment. One of those packaged things with equal parts of dried herbs and poisonous chemicals. Betty Crocker's Rice Galitzianer, perhaps. Sometimes I have fantasies of buying stone ground flour and organic vegetables and making everything from scratch, and then I cruise down the aisles at the Pathmark and fill the cart with all of this processed shit. I think there's something insidious about the pictures on the boxes. God knows nothing I make turns out looking like that. Even when they taste good they don't look like that.

The point being that dinner was a loser. After dinner he took a drink in to watch television by, like mood music. I followed at a distance. After the eleven o'clock news he turned to me. He was, I guess, about half in the bag. Half in the bag for Howie means he can still wiggle his toes if you give him a few minutes to work it all out in his mind.

Why am I being so bitchy?

Because I'm hostile.

Next question?

No, let's remember how this went. He said, "Jan, baby, this isn't working out, is it?"

A moment of panic. *What* wasn't working out? Our Vietnam policy? Our marriage? The new color television set? Rice Galitzianer?

"What I mean is that this is no way to start a family."

"Oh."

"You can't get pregnant watching television."

"Unless we do it doggie style." (I didn't say this. Like most good repartee, it occurred to me twelve hours after the moment when it would have been effective. What we all need is the opportunity to go over our lives with a blue pencil the next day.)

(And cross everything out? Maybe.)

"You know something, darling? I love you."

"And I love you, Howie."

"Baby, let's go upstairs."

"Sure, honey."

We live in a ranch house. Everything's on the same floor. One's speech patterns seem to derive from the culture in which one lives to the point where one summons one's bride unwittingly to the roof. I used to think, when Howie first invited me to an upstairs which wasn't there, that he had spent his childhood in a two-story house. Not so. He had never lived in a two-story house, had in fact never lived in a house before we moved to Eastchester. It was always an apartment somewhere or other in Brooklyn or the Bronx. When he and I had the apartment on Seventy-seventh Street, there was none of this *Let's go upstairs* cuteness. It came with the house, like the thirty-year mortgage and the leak in the basement and the army ants or whatever they are. Sometimes he catches himself, and sometimes I remind him, but it doesn't matter, he does it again the next time. Movies and books and television taught the poor man that when you live in a house you have to climb stairs to go to bed.

So we went upstairs—why fight it?—and went to bed, and he kissed me boozily and felt my breast—felt one of them, anyway—and thus inspired he gave a great sigh and passed out. *Went to sleep?* No. *Passed out* sums it up fine.

Leaving me to feel guilty about feeling glad.

I don't want a baby.

I guess I've never said that out loud. I guess most of the time I don't really believe it myself, but I do now. God, yes. I mean God, no.

I don't want a baby.

I wonder if he does, really. I don't think so. Men are supposed to have these undeniable impulses. I have a feeling they're as deniable as anything else. Mine certainly are.

You know what I think? I think it's all part of the image. Being a few years married, and past the honeymoon (God in heaven, are we ever past the honeymoon!) and having moved out of the crowded evil city and into the fresh (?) air of sweet suburbia. The car we bought, for example, is a station wagon. We never owned a car in New York—that was one of the things I hated about New York, you had to go through a big production whenever you wanted to go somewhere—and here we finally have a car, one car for the two of us, and what kind of car is it? A cute little sports car? A cunning and sensible compact? A big showy ostentatious ballsy sedan?

None of those things. A station wagon, a big klutzy station wagon with room for eighteen kids, none of which I want to have.

None of which I probably will have, having gone two years now without coming any closer to pregnancy than I don't know what. (You have a way with words, Giddings.)

And if I were using this book as a way of keeping compulsive records, rather than a place to jot down the observations of the moments (I think I mean *the observation of the moment,* both singular, although how few moments are *truly* singular, Doctor?) I might in that case feel compelled to state here in blue-black and white that in this year, now eight days old, we have, if memory serves, fucked once, and then not very well.

January 12

It snowed today. The snow that we already had was just about gone. For the past week or so it's been turning brown in the gutters, becoming slush, and bit by bit finding its way down the sewers. (You would almost think it was human.) So now it's snowing, coming down in big wet sticky flakes. I sat at the window and watched it and thought how beautiful it was, and how depressing.

Why is my first reaction to everything to think how much damned trouble it will be? Why don't I enjoy things?

January 14

Marcie Hillman thinks I should have an affair!

She came over this afternoon for the pause in the day's occupation she calls the housewife's hour, before her kids were due home from school. I made real coffee in honor of the occasion. The nice thing about instant coffee is that there is no way to screw it up. Not so with this afternoon's pot. You would think that after seven years of marriage I would know how to make a simple thing like a pot of coffee. You *would* think that, wouldn't you?

We sat in the kitchen and pretended the coffee was all right. And, like fighters warily circling one another in the opening round, we played *Who's Depressed?* (That's the first time I've named our game, but not the first time I've seen it as such. If there were a way to package it as a board game for two or more players, a way to introduce dice and spinners, I think it would outsell Scrabble.) We fence around, Marcie and I, alternately bubbly and sulking, until through some hard-to-follow process we mutually determine who will be patient and who will be therapist. The roles float back and forth from day to day and week to week. Her hang-ups are at least well defined, and I guess pretty standard. She keeps going on and off diets and forever weighs I guess twenty-five pounds more than she should. And she is periodically incapable of keeping her house as clean as she wants it, and never capable of keeping it as clean as Edgar wants it, Edgar being her husband. She is, for all of that, a tall and pretty blonde with a pretty if ample body. She is also a year and a half older than I am, which is to say that she is thirty, has in fact been thirty for a half a year, and it hasn't seemed to destroy her.

"You," she said, "are in a bad way."

"I suppose."

"What's the matter? The periodic distress of the female ilk?"

"Ilk? My periodic ilk isn't due for a week."

"And maybe you won't have it."

"Oh, I'll have it."

"You could be pregnant right now, kiddo. And then you'll glow with motherhood, and all the doubts and fears—"

"Oh, sure. Anyway, I'm not pregnant."

"I don't like to keep harping at it, but this one particular doctor is supposed to be fantastic. Every woman who goes to his office comes home pregnant."

"From his office?"

"I didn't say that exactly right."

"It sounded as if he screwed them himself."

"Well, whatever works, doll. American pragmatism in action. Better things for better living."

"Uh-huh. Who wants to be knocked up, anyway?"

"I thought you did."

"Maybe I don't."

"Oh?"

"Maybe I'm getting a little old for that sort of thing."

So we tossed the age pillow around for a little while, and other things, and then Marcie cocked her head—I think that's the word for it, set her head at an angle and swung her eyes at me—and told me I ought to have an affair.

"You know what?" she said. "You ought to have an affair."

"Just what I need."

"You think I'm kidding, don't you?"

"Well, aren't you?"

"No."

"Oh, for Christ's—"

"For your own sake, kiddo. Not J.C.'s. You're letting yourself go stale. Your whole marriage—do you mind home truths?"

"Go ahead."

"Right where the angels fear to tread. All right. I get the impression that you and what's-his-name are running out of each other. That it's all turning sour."

"That could be an exaggeration."

"Is it?"

"No."

"I didn't think so. But the thing is that it's more than your marriage. It's you. Do you know that it shows in your face?"

"What does?"

"The fact that you're bored all the time. That you're all drawn out, strained."

"I know. I can't stand to look in mirrors."

"Well, they ought to pass a law against mirrors. That's something else again."

"But I find myself looking into them all the time."

"Because you've forgotten who you are."

"Oh, come *on*—"

"A little trite, I grant you—"

"More than a little. Pure soap opera."

"—but no less true for a' that. Jan? Have you ever?"

"Ever what?"

"Had an affair?"

"No. Of course not."

"Uh-huh."

"You . . .?"

She smiled at a happy memory.

"You're not having one now?"

"Be serious. The way I look?"

We sidestepped into the *Oh, you don't look so bad/Oh, I'm so damn fat and what I wouldn't give for your figure* routine. But I was so taken with all of this that I almost forgot my lines. And she wouldn't say anything much about her affair, just that it had happened a couple of years ago, lasted a couple of months, and left her very happy about the whole thing.

"Was it with someone I know?"

"Now don't ask, Jan."

"That means it was. Did Edgar know the man?"

"Cut it out."

"Well, did Edgar ever find out about it?"

"No."

"What if he had?"

"Do you really think he would have minded all that much?" I must have stared incredulously, because she reacted to my expression. "Let's face it, honey. Edgar plays around."

"I didn't know that." This is not exactly true.

"Oh, of course. He's like a little boy, for God's sake. I think all men are. I'm positive he started fooling around before we were married two years."

"Well, who does he—"

"Girls at the office, tramps he picks up. There was a time, in my younger days, when I made scenes and threatened to leave. I laugh to think of it. I mean, where would I go?"

"But—"

"But what it amounts to is that something inside him makes him want that variety, and I can understand it most of the time, except when I start thinking that he wouldn't do it if I took off thirty pounds or got the ironing done or compensated for one or another of my many faults. But actually I don't think that would make any difference at all. I think he's simply the way he is. You know, he even makes passes at my friends. Has he ever made a play for you?"

"No." This wasn't exactly true, either. I can remember a couple of boozy kisses at a backyard barbecue, a tentative Grope for the Boobies while collecting the coats at another party. The bit at the barbecue had been merely annoying, but the other pass had come at a time when I felt myself slightly less attractive than Miss Hippopotamus, and while I might not welcome the grab, I welcomed the reassurance in the knowledge that Edgar Hillman thought I was still worth grabbing, an opinion that Howard Kurland had not at the moment appeared to share.

"You know," she said, a little later, "if you think Howard takes his marital vows so seriously, you're only kidding yourself."

"Are you trying to tell me something?"

"Nothing specific, no."

"Do you know something that I don't know?"

"Just that he's a man."

"And all men run around? I'm not positive I believe that. I've heard it often enough, but I'm not sure I believe it."

"Maybe not. But things haven't been going too well lately, have they?"

"Things have been going badly on and off for probably six out of the last seven years. Our marriage is like the country's foreign policy. We somehow muddle through."

"The country's foreign policy before Vietnam, you mean. Now we muddle, but not through."

"Fair enough. I don't see—"

"Okay." She pointed a finger at me. "Not all men run around. Some men have perfect marriages. Other men are profoundly unattractive, and other men lack the opportunity for an affair. Farmers who never get off the farm, for instance. But if a man's marriage is not the ranking love affair since Heloise and what's-his-name, and if he's got a certain amount of poise and looks and intelligence, and if he's got room to operate—"

"Uh-huh."

"And if, like most men, he tends to think with his penis—"

"You are describing Howard."

There was more, but that will do. My hand hurts. He called around dinner to say he was catching a late train. I had trouble not laughing until I put the phone down, and then for no particular reason I started crying instead. Real tears. My goodness, I hadn't cried in, oh, perhaps a day and a half.

The funny thing is that I have to admit I don't care if he's fucking Elizabeth Taylor, as far as that goes. I really don't care, and I suppose that was part of Marcie's point.

I don't know.

What do I want with an affair?

MY NEWSLETTER: I get out an email newsletter at unpredictable intervals, but rarely more often than every other week. I'll be happy to add you to the distribution list. A blank email to lawbloc@gmail.com with "newsletter" in the subject line will get you on the list, and a click of the "Unsubscribe" link will get you off it, should you ultimately decide you're happier without it.

LAWRENCE BLOCK is a Mystery Writers of America Grand Master. His work over the past half century has earned him multiple Edgar Allan Poe and Shamus awards, the U.K. Diamond Dagger for lifetime achievement, and recognition in Germany, France, Taiwan, and Japan. His latest novel is *Dead Girl Blues*; other recent fiction includes *A Time to Scatter Stones, Keller's Fedora*, and *The Burglar in Short Order*. In addition to novels and short fiction, he has written episodic television (*Tilt!*) and the Wong Kar-wai film, *My Blueberry Nights*.

Block contributed a fiction column in Writer's Digest for fourteen years, and has published several books for writers, including the classic *Telling Lies for Fun & Profit* and the updated and expanded *Writing the Novel from Plot to Print to Pixel*. His nonfiction has been collected in *The Crime of Our Lives* (about mystery fiction) and *Hunting Buffalo with Bent Nails* (about everything else). Most recently, his collection of columns about stamp collecting, *Generally Speaking*, has found a substantial audience throughout and far beyond the philatelic community.

Lawrence Block has lately found a new career as an anthologist (*At Home in the Dark; From Sea to Stormy Sea*) and holds the position of writer-in-residence at South Carolina's Newberry College. He is a modest and humble fellow, although you would never guess as much from this biographical note.

Email: lawbloc@gmail.com
Twitter: @LawrenceBlock
Facebook: lawrence.block
Website: lawrenceblock.com